THE RAPE OF A LOCK

LEO ALEXANDER SAKHAROV

Copyright © 2020 by Leo Alexander Sakharov

All rights reserved.

No part of this book may be reproduced in any form or by any electronic or mechanical means, including information storage and retrieval systems, without written permission from the author, except for the use of brief quotations in a book review.

❦ Created with Vellum

For my Family

INTRODUCTION

I started writing this book to address a common theme that has plagued humanity for thousands of years: the oppression of women. From life in Greece or Rome when a woman could not leave her house without the accompaniment of a male counterpart; to the Spanish Inquisition when the Catholic Church attempted to subjugate all freethinking and independent women in Europe; to the Salem Witch Trials in the New World when freethinking and independent women faced, yet again, oppression and subjugation by a male dominated society; women have had to endure more oppression than almost anyone else on earth.

The planet created all life on Earth. And women gave birth to every single human being on the entire planet. That is simply nature and biology. Until we as a human race fundamentally respect all women as the mothers of our children, we will never create a world of justice and peace.

If you ever doubted the power of women, just remember, if women stopped having sex with men, and giving birth to children, for a single generation, the entire human race would go extinct. That is the power of women.

I can only hope that more free and independent women continue to stand up to their male oppressors and hopefully one day this paternal society will finally end and we will create a more equal society in its place. I think we could solve most of the world's problems simply by doing that.

The only problem we face is that the men who struggle to keep themselves in power and control over the entire world are deathly afraid of what free and independent women will do if they were the ones in control. Maybe they should be afraid.

I hope you enjoy the book.

1

"I love her. My heart is dying to have her."

The music played as I dumbly felt for the lock pick trying to fit it into the keyhole. Sweat poured off my brow and ran down my nose before dripping onto the dusty floor of the cellar. The furnace billowed heat, so cloying, smothering me in its embrace. I could barely see my hands in front of me in the dim, pale light of the moon that entered from the door at the top of the stairs. I was beyond fear. I was beyond temptation. I had to have her. I was desperate to have her or else lose my sanity.

Sealed in her vault, she danced. I could hear her laughing. I could smell her perfume. All I could see was the pale beam of pink and purple light drifting out from the keyhole. She was on the other side.

Madly, I pounded the intolerable door. I spat at the impenetrable lock. And I shrieked at the top of my lungs, "I must have you!" into the distant echoes of the night. I cried as I vainly fit pick to lock again and again, trying to turn the tumbler, to free the door, and gain entry into her paradise; her forbidden Eden. It was there I wanted to dwell. It was there I wanted to spend the rest of my life; with her. My hands trembled and I dripped with sweat, teeth clenched, fumbling in the dark.

~

It all began two summers ago when I acquired this home. I work for a prominent architectural firm in London. Quite an historic agency, really. And quite fitting to the history of the company, my profession is historic restoration, a service my company is widely reputed for in its excellence in doing. I was chief of staff in my division, working mainly on large commercial projects: museums, hospitals, and universities. Sometimes our firm would acquire an odd urban dwelling, some private building, or home. The company was in the habit of purchasing properties of exceptional condition and either restoring them and declaring them historic sites, or modernizing them and selling them on the market.

Chad Braughburn was the head negotiator for acquisitions, a dear friend and colleague. He and I started in the company together more than two decades ago; he specializing in finance and property value and I in historic and architectural integrity. Together we made quite a team. Chad would often get rift of a property of purported historical worth and I would go out and assess the property with a team of engineers.

Sometimes we floundered, but mostly we were on the up and up, acquiring great properties and earning great commissions. It was on such an occasion that we came across this house, an 18th century Georgian home in remarkable condition. Indeed, it was everything I had ever dreamed of in a home. At the time, I didn't quite get the pun when Chad cheekily asked me to assess its condition. 'Don't fall in love, the contract isn't signed yet,' he said and laughed. But when I saw the home, I understood completely.

I've always wanted a proper Georgian home and Chad knew this. He knew this dream of mine as well as I did we had talked of it so often. 'When I have my home, we'll have you and yours over as often as possible for dinner parties. We'll play billiards and drink Scotch…' so on and so forth. He being married and with three children, knew of my solitary lifestyle, and wished a life for me with a wife and child. He and I loved each other very much and would do anything possible for each other. Such pure friendship was rare and we knew it.

Chad was negotiating the acquisition of the property from a smaller company who found they didn't possess the resources necessary to properly restore the home, as often happens when a young, ambitious company latches onto a find that is beyond their ability to manage. They marked it up a nominal fee, but according to Chad, if the home proved to be truly historic and structurally sound, it would be well worth the investment.

When I first saw the home, I fell in love with it immediately. It was the picture of perfection; from its pleasant spot on the row beyond the commons; to the immaculate garden that adorned the courtyard. It was the picture of elegance. My grandmother had always fancied me a gentleman. She would call me a little gentleman at every Christmas holiday. She applauded my considerate manner and I loved her for it. 'You are such a gentleman!' she would say about my manners at the table and I beamed with joy. My family hadn't much, in fact we were quite poor, and to be called a gentleman filled me with pride. In the age of grace, when a man had acquired the station of gentleman, he would often reside in a domestic Georgian home. Such was the home I dreamed of.

When I first visited the home, I knew right away that Chad would make his investment in earnest. This was an absolutely pristine Georgian home, down to the carved stone cornices adorning the copper chute and gutter at either side of the façade. The authenticity of the home was unmistakable.

From the street it appeared to be completely intact. The house retained its broad square shape; no exterior modifications or additions, except for the addition of a small portico over the front door. Two large, rectangular windows bordered in a dark teal blue casing adorned the façade on either side of the front entrance. The second floor had four large windows the same as the lower. Separating them, placed above the door, was an oval mosaic of glass.

The heavy oak front door, painted a subtle grey, was bordered with hardwood casings and set into a cut stone entry. The house itself was made entirely of grey brick and rest on a massive foundation of cut stone.

The roof, prominent with its small, trapezoidal rise at the center, a dark, almost blackish grey, decorated with a small, iron storm fence. Four chimneys for eight fireplaces; four on each floor. Two steps up to the front door and the landing; quite traditional in Georgian homes. The landing quite small; no more than 2 meters square.

The home itself was magnificent, solid, massive, and elegant. With the courtyard it was simply exquisite. The courtyard was lined with hedges. A flowerbed adorned the front of the house on either side of the landing. A miniature pine flanked each side at the corners of the home. A light brown gravel path wound its way from the front gate to the porch in a delicate "S" curve. A birdbath rest in the center of the left side of the courtyard and a high lattice, covered in ivy, separated the front courtyard from the side patio at the left corner of the house. There was an arched gate at the right corner of the house leading to the back of the property.

I sent the structural engineers inside to go forward with the inspection of the foundation, floor joists, and exterior walls. Roofs almost always suffer some damage and I felt it best to inspect that last as it would be tedious and time-consuming. I stayed outside admiring the home. Could this be the one? The home I would raise my family in?

On either side of the home were two large commercial buildings. The home was nestled in between, making it seem quite out of place. I couldn't help but to feel that the home had somehow been placed in a time machine and preserved, kept free from harm, until now, and was placed here solely for my benefit. It seemed so amazing.

I walked back and forth on the pavement in front of the house, running my hand along the top of the wrought iron fence that surrounded the property. 'Impeccable,' I thought. The fence was a 19th century addition, very well done. Iron fence with hewn stone pillars spaced every three meters. Heavy stone pillars on either side of the gate. The gate adorned with a decorative iron arch, in which laid the word, "Tasslebury."

It seemed a cemetery entrance, or some gate to an enchanted wood or forest in some fairy tale. I ran my fingers across the metal of the arch. A light dusting of rust drifted down onto my shoulder. It was fairy dust I mused. Suddenly, I was so taken aback that I stepped back into the street with my arms outstretched and heaved an immense sigh, as if all of my dreams had been answered. I breathed it in. My home. At least, I hoped.

I earn a salary, but also a commission on larger, more

prominent projects. I had been saving my commissions to buy a home, when I found it. After my last commission, the structural restoration of a museum, the completion of which awarded me an additional £15,000, I had over £750,000; quite a hefty sum. I decided to speak with Chad about acquiring the home for myself.

"It's worth the acquisition then?" Chad was very excited, for me perhaps.

"It is a beautiful home. It's everything I've ever wanted in a home."

"A bit out of your range, though."

It was set at £1,250,000 in its present condition.

"I have enough to make a substantial down payment and make a bid for the home."

"Not necessary. I've drawn up the papers, just in case, and the company will hold the property in lien during its restoration where it will then be set for bid starting at £2,000,000."

"Two million? That high?"

"Yes, I'm afraid so. But, that's just the standard paperwork. I've drawn up, for ourselves, a proprietary contract where the company would continue to hold the house in lien for twenty years and carry the balance of the initial investment while *you* lead the restoration and make use of it as your personal home."

"How is that legal?"

"Everything is legal as to the holdings of the deed to the home. I conferred with the legal department. The company can hold the property in lien for you and allow you the time to accumulate the necessary deposits to buy it outright. The only negotiable infraction is that you would be getting paid to lead the restoration of your future home, on company time, with company resources. That, I'm afraid, is a bit shady."

"But I could bid for the house now at £1,250,000 and do the restoration myself as I intended."

"Yes that's just how it's drawn up; for the value of the home in its present condition. That's the sum the contract sets as its price. Look, I've talked to the partners. We all love you here. You've made us famous and we would be despairingly poor mannered if we let this one go by without lending you a hand. We've negotiated a separate contract, whereby you would restore the home, using company resources, and you would be accountable for costs plus 4%. However expensive the restoration is will be entirely up to you as you are the beneficiary of the contract."

"I don't know what to say. I'm overwhelmed!"

"There is one stipulation, however." He added crossing to the cabinet to pour a couple of Scotches. I became weary at the gravity of his tone. He turned and crossed to me and in all severity said:

"Your home is to be used yearly, for the company Christmas party for the life of the loan." Then he smiled, gave me a tearful hug and passed me a drink. "Congratulations old man! You're a proper gentleman!"

~

I had to swallow my drink before I mentioned it. I don't know why I dreaded it, why I was so fearful, but it held a mystery I could not grasp.

"Um… Chad. There's something I didn't mention. It's in my report, of course, but there's something in the cellar; a room that I wasn't able to survey."

"Is that right? What of it? Will it deter you from purchasing the home?"

"No, no. Nothing like that. I'm sure the foundation is intact. It's just that, well, it's barred by this enormous door.

It's locked tight; more than tight; it's completely sealed. The door... the door itself is massive. Well not as large in dimension as in weight. It must be a foot thick. Built of huge hewn timbers banded together by heavy iron straps. It looks as if it had come out of some medieval dungeon."

He saw the look of dread in my eyes and chortled out:

"Ooh! Ghosts in the dungeon have we?" Then he burst out laughing.

I smiled back and took another drink. I have to admit I was a bit perplexed. I didn't know why I was so fascinated and afraid of that door. It just seemed to hold some impending doom. I couldn't figure it out. I didn't know why I felt this way, but it had something to do with the way the door was made. I continued with my explanation.

"While I was at the house, after the engineers had finished with the cellar and gone on to inspect the upper floors and I was busy inspecting the furnace, I felt something; something very cold; not quite like a breeze, but something more. I turned the instant I felt it and knew exactly where it had come from. It had come from the door. Then I recognized what it was that I felt. It was as if *the door* had taken a deep breath. I was numb with fear, but I couldn't believe that's what it was, so I crossed to the door and began to inspect it more closely.

"The door is located about a meter from the bottom of the stairs leading into the cellar, just to the left as you come down and before you get to the furnace, which sits near the front of the house directly under the foyer. The chamber behind the door would be under the parlor.

"The foundation wall is composed of massive cut stones fitted and jointed together like a Roman coliseum. The archway for the door, just over two meters square, is built right into the foundation with blocks of stone on either side of the opening and an arch with a keystone at the top.

"The door itself is perfectly fit to the opening allowing no light to pass between the door and the jamb. The door must swing in and the front edges of the door meet flush with the opening, leaving not even a hair's breadth all the way around. At the foot, a row of stone blocks sealed the bottom edge.

"The door itself was so blackened with soot that it almost glistened in the light. The timbers were so dense, so solid, and so massive that they must have been petrified. All of the timbers were jointed and fitted leaving no space between them. And the wide iron bands that bound them together were each more than a quarter inch think and nearly a foot wide; one across the top and another at the bottom.

"On the right, mounted to the door, were a heavy iron plate with an iron pull ring, and below the pull ring was a large keyhole. All of the nails in the door were filed down so that you could not remove them. They lay flush with the surface of the iron bands. There was no way to remove any part of the door or the lock, except the pull ring, from the outside.

"I felt the edges of the keyhole with my fingers and tried to peer through it into the blackness. Although I couldn't see anything, I felt something move. Like a shadow blown in the breeze. Then the door itself breathed again and I dropped whatever was in my hand, fell back onto my haunches, and back peddled across the floor.

"I don't know how long I stared at it, its massive blackness, but I swear I could see swirls of black smoke floating and drifting in front of it. I was mesmerized with fear. Then one of the engineers called out to me, I snapped out of it, and ran upstairs."

"Andrew Martin." Chad seemed quite stern. I was perplexed by his tone. "Are you being purposefully cheeky? I have never known you to be either timid or superstitious.

Don't tell me you've gotten cold feet just as you were offered the house of your dreams? I wouldn't know what to tell Betsy after all we've done to make this deal happen."

Of course, he was right. I had no right to seem so ungrateful. I was, on the contrary, extremely grateful; more than grateful. I don't know what it was I felt. I tried not to let it show.

"Of course, I am grateful. And moreover, I am deeply humbled to have such wonderful friends. Cheers!" And we warmed ourselves over a couple of tumblers of Scotch.

∽

We began the restoration in the fall, three months later. I set up a temporary office in the study. A table made of two sawhorses and a sheet of plywood served as my desk. I laid all of the house plans on it and directed most of the work from there while I sipped from a coffee mug.

I decided to start with a general stripping and cleaning to determine what the surface condition of the house was like before we got into any heavy renovations. I was busy studying the electrical and plumbing plans.

Historic restoration does not, of course, mean that we rely on centuries old technology, but rather that we incorporate modern technologies into the historical aesthetic of the home. All of the electrical and plumbing would be removed and replaced.

According to the plans, at one time the home was fitted with natural gas light. I hoped the remnants of the system was still there so that I might make use of gas lighting in certain areas of the house; the hallway sconces, the foyer, and the front porch predominantly. I couldn't help but to grin as I looked over the plans.

The first floor of the home was comprised of six rooms

including the foyer, which was positioned in the center of the house at the front. The staircase lay in the foyer 10 feet ahead of the front door and to the right. They led straight back and up to the second floor landing which overlooked the foyer below.

At the back of the foyer, on the left, was an entrance to the kitchen. At the foot of the stairs, to the right, lay the entry into the front parlor. A large opening that could accommodate many persons entering and leaving, to sit or to venture about. In the parlor, a fireplace adorned the wall opposite the entry, flanked by two large windows. And two large windows occupied the front. The back wall held a pair of French doors which opened into the dining room.

The dining room was large with a fireplace centered on the outside wall, again flanked by two large windows. An entry from the kitchen lay at the back left, another from the foyer, below the landing. Another pair of French doors filled the back wall and opened into a sunroom or antechamber at the back of the house.

On the opposite side of the foyer from the parlor lay the master study. The entry to the study paralleled the entry to the parlor and was framed with a heavy, lacquered oak frame with an equally heavy oak door. Inside the study, to the left, within the front wall, lay the front windows, which looked out onto the front courtyard. Opposite the entry were a pair of French doors which opened onto the side courtyard. A large fireplace filled the exterior wall towards the back of the room. Bookcases and mahogany panels with a delicate inlay adorned the walls on every side of the room. The back wall, again, held a pair of French doors that opened into the billiard room.

Another fireplace was in the billiard room, flanked by two large windows, mirroring that in the dining room. A door to the right led back into the foyer. Another at the back, led to the kitchen. A small bar occupied the right side wall.

Central to the house, adjoining both the billiard and the dining rooms was the kitchen. The kitchen was quite spacious. Towards the front of the house lay most of the appliances and the sink. An island stove filled the center of the room. At the back of the room was a breakfast table, beyond which two sets of French doors opened onto the back patio. Outside was a small yard, and at the back to the right was the carriage house and drive leading to the street. The garden was well maintained and quite beautiful.

Upstairs above the study lay a large guest bedroom. The master bedroom lay above the billiard room. Above the kitchen lay the master bath.

On the opposite side, there was another large guest room over the parlor, and one small guest room over the dining room. Both were separated by a large linen closet, inside which lay a winding staircase that led up and into the attic.

A separate washroom shared space with the master bath over the kitchen. Servants' quarters were in the attic, utilities and storage in the cellar. All very comfortable and cozy.

∽

I worked on the home for about three months before I decided to pack a few things in case I needed to stay the night on the premises. I had a small bed and some linens placed in the guest room located above the parlor as the work continued.

The general stripping and cleaning was completed in the first couple of months. We had moved on to the next step of the process which was an exploratory search of all of the walls, floors, and ceilings to make sure that all of the internal structures were intact.

We, unfortunately, uncovered quite a bit of wood rot in the walls, mostly in areas with plumbing and, of course, with the modernization the house had undergone over the years, several wall studs were cut into to allow for gas piping and electrical wiring. It wasn't nearly as bad as it could have been, and the good thing was we were able to salvage enough of the natural gas lines that were left in the walls to reuse them in the renovation.

The roof was altogether another story. It had been repaired at least a few times and for the most part they did a fairly good job at it, but there were some major repairs needed requiring the replacement of several beams, practically rebuilding the entire southwest corner. But these things are to be expected in a project like this. It's delicate work.

Most of the walls were plastered and in order to explore the walls and assess the damage, we had to remove some of the plaster. Most of the plaster and the wooden slats underneath, of course, would be preserved.

Remarkably, most of the joists in the basement and the ceiling were completely intact. The foundation only needed to be sand blasted and weather sealed. The furnace I decided to keep as it had been refitted with gas and had quite an intrinsic value. All in all, the project was moving along quite well and within a couple of month's time we would have everything structural properly assessed and ready to begin the delicate and time consuming removal of the electrical and plumbing systems.

∼

I tried not to think about what happened when I first encountered the door in the cellar. I simply put it out of my mind and went about the task at hand. I had decided it was best just never to speak of it. But as work continued on schedule in the upper floors of the house, work was a bit stymied in the cellar, specifically in regards to that door.

The problem was that there was just no way to breach the opening. I called a locksmith and a blacksmith to come and take a look at the door. I had a couple of the engineers look at it as well, but no solution could be found aside from destroying the door and tearing it out, which, for reasons of historic preservation, I absolutely refused to do. It had become a wonder to me.

The locksmith could do nothing. He came back several times, every time with new equipment and devices, and every time telling me that unless I would allow him to cut into the lock mechanism and tear into the timbers there was nothing he could do. I must admit part of the reason I did not allow him to do so was because I was afraid of what might come out.

The blacksmith was of no better help than the locksmith. He did however explain to me that the nails binding the iron bands to the timber were driven into the wood, countersunk into the metal bands, and then sealed with molten iron, fusing the entire assembly together. And that unless I wanted to cut through the metal with a high powered saw and break through the door with a ram there was no way for him to remove the door.

The engineers advised me not to disturb the foundation in any significant way, so cutting the stone or burrowing through were out of the question. I personally did not want to try to chisel away at the opening or the arch for fear that this would create undo stress around the opening and weaken the integrity of the foundation.

That door had become both a major thorn in my side and a very curious enigma. So, after much deliberation and trepidation, I decided to let it be for the time being and to simply continue with the rest of the house.

∽

We had our annual Christmas party at the office. I know Chad had chided me about having it in my new home, but we knew full well that it was company tradition to have the Christmas party at the office and this year was no different.

We ended the day early and busted out the bubbly. My assistant, Shelly, was leaning against the copy machine in her white blouse and red skirt, long blond hair, and big round mouth, singing show tunes with Earl the copy boy. Chad was with his wife Betsy, drinking some champagne and softly singing along. He seemed quite happy with his wife leaning against his chest and equally as content to stand quietly in the doorway to his office somewhat removed from the rest of the festivities. Matthew, our 70-year-old clerk, was drunk and acting the fool with a party hat on his head and a whistle blower in his mouth, dancing around the room like a twelve-year-old schoolboy. About ten of us in all cajoled together for a good three hours or so.

Shelly, lovely woman, was always trying to set me up on dates with her friends, or strangers for that matter. Sometimes it was someone she had just met, but just knew was perfect for me. I tried never to go, never to get mixed up in these 'dates,' but sometimes Shelly could be quite tenacious, and every so often, possibly out of desperation and loneliness, I would acquiesce and go along on one of these adventures.

The last woman Shelly introduced me to was a beautiful, intelligent single mother with a very lovely boy of about seven. She was quite charming and although I liked her very much as a person, I just could not see myself in a serious relationship with her and the thought of having casual sex with a single mother was just beyond me. I gave up after three dates and told her we should just be friends. She hasn't called back since.

This time, Shelly brought a member of her monthly reading group, Anna, to the Christmas party and was tactfully trying to pawn her off onto me. I tried, as politely as I could, to maintain a civil and pleasant level of conversation, but Shelly made it a habit of poking her nose into our conversation and encouraging either Anna or myself to "get to know the other a little better."

Of course, this only exasperated an already uncomfortable situation and a quiet lull developed in the conversation. I simply conveyed my wishes to Anna that we try to remain friends, or, in the very least, acquaintances. I don't think that bode well with her. She simply removed herself from the conversation and I didn't see her for the rest of the evening.

I began to feel rather depressed and lonely at the Christmas party. Like I was alone in a room full of friends, so I quietly made my exit without saying goodbye. I thought I'd spend my first, solitary Christmas in my future home.

I arrived at the house at about a quarter to nine. When I stepped into the home, standing just inside the foyer, the room lit only by the streetlights outside, I felt as if I were in a dream. I turned on the lights and, as if on cue, a drama began before my eyes as I imagined the house filled with guests, all in vintage regalia.

The women wore little feathered masks and silky black dresses; their lashes incredibly long and their eyes incredibly dark. Gin and Highballs were passed around as a Rag Time band played in the study. Gentlemen in black tuxedos, jackets unbuttoned, played billiards and smoked cigars while flapper girls sat on top of the bar, poised for seductive indulgences smoking cigarettes from long, black stems.

The cooks and housemaids in the kitchen boiled lobster and prepared salads at rapid pace. In the upstairs nursery, a few ladies passed a baby girl amongst themselves. A few party strays, tempted by the smell of the appetizers, wandered into the dining room to help themselves to the small strawberry and chocolate aperitifs placed at the table, the ones that were to be reserved for the opening toast.

In the front parlor, a fire burned in the fireplace and a small gathering of people engaged in elegant conversation. The ambiance of this room was so removed from the rest of the house that I was immediately drawn to it. I unconsciously began walking into the parlor.

A couple of ladies in black satin dresses sat on a divan in front of the windows while a gentleman in a tuxedo stood beside them talking. He was incredibly sophisticated; his blond hair slicked back in a perfect sheen of gold. Then he turned his head and addressed someone hidden behind the back of a chaise lounge that sat in front of the fireplace.

A woman's soothing, commanding voice answered back and I saw her arm rise above the back of the chaise in a bit of whimsy and fortitude. She spoke with a soft, delicate, but powerful voice full of confidence and bold self-assurance. I didn't hear what she said. I only heard the tone and temperament of her voice.

Then a car's headlights shone through the front windows and woke me from my trance. I realized that I was standing in an empty room, wearing my trench coat and carrying my briefcase, my right hand poised to touch the back of the chaise lounge and look over.

"What am I doing?" I mumbled to myself. "I'm a waking somnambulist!"

I walked back into the foyer, removed my coat, and went upstairs to go to bed. I turned at the top of the landing, looked back down towards the parlor, and mused to myself, 'Christmas parties!' and turned out the lights.

∽

I went to bed anticipating a relaxing evening of cat stretches and pleasant dreams. I awoke in the middle of the night, my body numbed by the cold, and realized that the furnace had gone out.

I grabbed the torchlight and headed downstairs to the cellar wearing my pajamas and slippers. It was even colder in the cellar. Frost had formed on the stone walls of the foundation. I had no idea what I was doing. I searched the furnace and tried to find the pilot light to no avail. I tried to open a door or remove a panel, but had no idea what I would find if I did. So I pounded the top of the furnace with my fist and when that didn't work I kicked it a couple of times with the flat of my foot.

"Come on!" I cried, as if by coaxing the furnace would fire back up.

I was about to throw the damned torch at it when, through the thickness of the cold, I heard a moan. I spun around on my heels and thrust my torchlight in the direction the sound had come from. Where I thought it had come from.

A slow mist fell from the blackened door. I could see it glistening in the moonlight. I could hear the delicate hiss of it falling to the floor as it wafted through the air. The moon was just bright enough to cast a pale glow from the top of the stairs. My teeth chattered in the cold. The ancient blackness of the door stared back at me.

I swear I heard a moan. Not a frightening moan. It was almost pleasant, like a woman just waking in the morning. It might have been pleasant had it any reason to be there at all. A loud thud emanated from the density of the timbers, so powerful that the iron ring above the lock shook. Then again, the soft moan of a woman. I stood there paralyzed.

Was that really what I heard? It was so faint, yet so clear. I began to shiver from fear. The black mass stared back at me like the face of corporeal death. It was horrifying. The door seemed to breath, the frost glistening on its surface. Then I felt… something. A wisp of shadow ran up my arm, flew through the air, and encircled me. I dropped my torchlight and ran up the stairs, tripping on the way up. Once at the top, I slammed the cellar door shut and threw the bolt.

I was so panicked that I nearly choked. My God, what was down there? I tried to collect myself, pulling my hair back with my fingers. The glow of the moon shone on me through the foyer window. I swore I had heard the faint sound of a moan. I took another step back from the door. I was petrified. Was it a ghost? Was I mad?

I ran into the kitchen. Boxes and newspapers and buckets of plaster lay everywhere. The cabinets and counter tops covered by tarpaulin. I bit my nails and wondered what to do. I could call Chad. No. It's late, much too late to wake him. It was nearly 4:00am. No repairman would be available at this hour. I calmed myself and forced myself to be rational. I was too old to act like a frightened child. I decided to go back upstairs, wrap myself in my blankets, and wait until morning. Once calmed, I would be able to rationally explain what it was that I felt.

I quietly huddled on top of my bed and buried myself beneath my blankets. Before long I drifted into a haze somewhere between wakefulness and sleep. Shortly thereafter, I fell into a deep slumber.

In my sleep I began to hear the faint sound of music. It was almost inaudible at first, then it gradually grew louder; just loud enough that I could tell what it was: an old recording of Rag Time played on a Victrola. You could hear the pop and hiss of the needle as the record spun on its turntable. I heard the words:

"It seems like a year, since I've seen you dear, yet I know it's been only a day. Yet the hours seem long and the world goes wrong for it's empty with you away... And I wake from each dream of your loveliness, to sink once again into loneliness, and I'd give all the world for just one caress, I'm lonesome, I guess, that's all!"

In my mind's eye I saw the Victrola. Then I saw a slender arm reach in and wind the crank. I began to rouse from my slumber. The music still played. I slowly opened my eyes and panned the room. It was still before dawn. The room lay bare except for the bed I was on and the trunk that held my possessions. The wide eyes of the windows stared back at me. The sound of music filled my ears in faint echoes. It was beautiful and melodic. I was hypnotized by its sound.

Suddenly, I realized that I was awake and could still hear the music. A cold chill ran down my spine. I leapt from the bed and searched the room. Where was this music coming from? I remembered the shadow that encircled me and cried out:

"What are you?"

The music grew louder. I could hear the faint echo of metal on metal. A slow beating rhythm that nearly matched my heartbeat as I paced the room. The sound came from somewhere low. I could hear it echo as if it were coming from some deep chamber. I followed the sound to the wall near the bed and it grew louder. I pushed the bed to one side and found a heat register. I could hear the music emanating from the heat register, drifting up from the cellar. I thought of the door glistening with frost and terror gripped me. I wanted to rip the register grate from the wall! Anything to stop this ghostly music from funneling into my head.

"What do you want?" I whispered.

The rhythmic beat of metal on metal grew louder. The sound began to leave the room and, instead, to fill my head in echoes and swirls. It began to pulse and grow louder until my head was throbbing with it. Then, in the midst of the cacophony, there she was, a woman… laughing. Not a shrill laugh, nor a frightening one, but the soft, gentle laugh of a woman; almost playful. 'Are you laughing at me?' I thought. And the rapacious rhythm of metal, music and laughter rose to a deafening roar within my head.

"Are you laughing at me?" I yelled.

Silence. It all stopped. All at once. I was alone with my breathing and the timpani of my heartbeat. Dawn broke over the horizon and the first rays of the sun drifted into the room through the windows.

∼

I decided to dress and take the train to the office. Before I left, in the safety of the morning light, I decided to check the latch on the cellar door. The house was quiet. My breath left little clouds in the air. I made my way down the stairs and into the foyer. It was an unbelievable sight. The sun shone through the windows, coloring the entire house in gold. Everything shimmered in luminescence. Faint traces of mist circled through the air.

I could barely bring myself to walk through the foyer. I

avoided the parlor and the dining room. I, instead, passed through the study and the billiard room into the kitchen. I stood inside the kitchen and looked through the doorway, across the foyer, and at the door to the cellar. It was impossible for me to get any closer. I inspected the latch from a distance and hoped that whatever was down there was safely contained down there. Then I wondered why a latch would make any difference at all.

My crew would not be able to work without heat. I decided to call everyone and tell them to take the day off. Then I grabbed my things and headed to the office.

As I was leaving, I stood in front of the house for a few moments. The front of the house faces east and the morning sun lit on the windows. It looked so serene, so peaceful, with its cemetery gate: "Tasslebury."

I had only done the architectural research on the home: blueprints, construction documents, etc. I hadn't researched its history. I would have to do so. Was this a haunting? Was there even such a thing?

I phoned the repairman from the office. He would meet me at 5 o'clock that evening. I kept wondering why the hell I was so damned terrified. It couldn't possibly have been a woman, or a ghost. It must have been the pipes, or the furnace letting out a hiss. Something fell in the attic and that's the thump I heard that shook the iron ring. I was still drunk from the Christmas party. Anything. But it could not have been what I thought it was; what I swore it was. Whatever I felt fly around and encircle me, it wasn't a spirit, it wasn't.

And although it had so terrified me, that voice and that music were so pleasant, so warm, so beautiful. If it had not been for the fact that they had no right to be there at all, I would have found them inviting, even sensual. I had to get the thoughts out of my mind. The repairman would be there at five. I would not arrive back home until a quarter to. I had no intention of going back down there alone, as crazy as that sounds.

I spent the day at the office pulling every drawing I could find on the home. There must be some way to breach that door. I had no idea where to begin looking. I studied all of the architectural plans that I could find. I knew there had to be a clue hidden somewhere in one of the drawings and that there must be some way of knowing how long that door in the cellar had been sealed shut. Whatever the answers, they lay buried behind that door. That much I was certain. I searched all of the plans we possessed, but found nothing. Before I knew it, it was after 4 o'clock. I had to meet the repairman.

I arrived at the home at a quarter to five and waited on the landing, outside in the cold. I blew warm air into my hands and stomped my feet. There was a bitter chill in the air. After I'd had enough, I worked up the nerve to open the front door and peer inside. It was dark and lonely, with barely enough light to see through the foyer.

The supplies and tools in the study and in the parlor were just shadows. It was now past 5 o'clock. I stepped inside and turned on the light. I shook out my coat and looked into the parlor. Drop cloths and buckets and tools lay everywhere. We were preparing to remove the plumbing and electrical systems. Temporary lighting had been strung in every room. The light from the foyer only lit half the room. I took a few rather timid steps towards the parlor.

"Hello?" a voice called out.

I jumped through the roof within my skin and my heart skipped a beat.

"My God, you gave me a fright!"

The repairman had come up behind me.

"Didn't mean to scare ya. Door was open. Thought I'd

come in out of the cold. Name's Dermot" He put out a hand.

He was an elderly gentlemen of about 60, but still fit by the looks of it. I took his hand and shook it.

"Oh, Andrew. Pleasure to meet you. I'm afraid it's not much warmer in here. Please, come in. The cellar's this way, under the stairs."

"Very nice home you have here."

"Yes it is. It is a beautiful home. Are you sure the door wasn't closed? It's not like me to…"

"As open as a barn door, mate," he smiled back.

"I see. Well, this house has been a dream of mine for years and now that I have it, I'm restoring it to period."

"Very proud. Very proud, indeed."

"Well, the furnace is in the cellar and it has been modified to support natural gas. The casing is original, but the equipment has been replaced and modernized…"

" Ginny."

"Pardon?"

"Your furnace's name is Ginny. I've been in here a time or two and am quite familiar with ol' Ginny."

"I see. You name them do you?"

"Only the old ones like Ginny here. A classic machine she is. Helps me to keep the houses organized."

"Then you should know how to fix it… her then, right?"

"I think I know what the problem is. We'll see once I have a closer look."

I tried to see my torchlight from the top of the stairs, but its eye was cold and dark. The batteries must have worn out.

"There's no light in the cellar. I apologize. I forgot to mention it. We're in the process of upgrading."

"That's quite alright, I have a rather large work light right here."

He produced a large, round halogen lamp, which, when he turned it on, lit the very corners of the room. I thought of accompanying Dermot into the cellar, then I thought better of it.

"Well, there you are. I'm sure you can find your way," I said, feigning politeness.

"Yes sir. Thank you very much," he answered.

As he descended into the pitch, I suddenly felt I should warn him, but caught myself. I shook my head mulling over what foolishness I had been catering to. I stayed at the top of the stairs and every so often glimpsed at the blackness of the door, just sitting there, so heavy, so monstrous.

The fright of the door is what caught me. I had so completely convinced myself that it must be some gate to hell that I was completely spooked just looking at it. I had to come to my senses. It was only a door. One day I would have it opened, get all of the skeletons out of the closet, and be done with it. Still, just the sight of it seemed to suck all of the courage right out of me. I had to look away. I decided it was safer to stand nearer the repairman, so I went down and stood next to Dermot.

"So, do you think you can fix it?" I said.

"The furnace and the blower look fine. The lines and fittings are fine as well. It looks like the jets are the cause of the problem. Sediment and rust have been collecting in these jets for quite some time. They're clogged shut. You're lucky they're clogged and not filling the air with gas. Otherwise you could've blown your beautiful home sky high. You'll need to replace the gas lines and jets if you want this done right. I can come back in a week with the parts and do the job properly. For now, I can just clean them out. It will take me an hour or so, but you should be sleeping very warm and toasty tonight."

"Thank you. That's very good to hear. You seem to like

ol' Ginny here. How would you like to do a full refurbishment on her?"

"Pardon?"

"A full stripping and cleaning; rebuilding and refitting as necessary. Of course, I'd like to maintain the original furnace and as much of the original equipment as I can, but I'm going to need a proper heating system. I think you're just the man for the job."

"I am mighty grateful that you think so, sir. That is quite a bit of work; at least a couple of weeks, maybe more; quite expensive as well. Parts, original parts, aren't easy to come by, ya know."

"Yes I do, I know very well. And I believe you know a lot about this furnace. So, what do you say? Shall we sign a contract?"

"Why, yes sir. Thank you. Thank you very much. If that's the case, you might want me to replace all of the ductwork in the house. My father was the one who put it in. I'm sure it could use replacing by now."

"Well, then it is my honor and privilege to meet you. We've inspected the entire house's internal structure including all of the utilities and I am very grateful that your father was able to run the ductwork between lines without damaging too much of the superstructure."

"What are you an architect?" he said.

"I actually work for a firm," I said. "We're restoring the entire home to period. We've just assessed the property and your father's work was very clean and well appreciated among us."

"Well thank you, sir," he said. "That is very good to hear. It's nice to know his work is appreciated."

"Well, I expect 'ol Ginny will be well cared for then."

As I answered, I watched the door out of the corner of my eye, the light shimmering on its surface. I felt a beat emanate from it, a pounding like the beating of a heart. My eyes widened. 'I'm inside,' it whispered.

I fought myself not to jump with fright. Not in front of Dermot. But, I had to back away towards the stairs. Dermot went back to doing the repairs and knelt in front of the furnace just a couple of meters further in. The door stood between he and I.

I suddenly thought of the empty blackness that lay beyond the door and out of that blackness I imagined a cruel and hideous creature of shadow and smoke coming after me. I could not contain my fear. I slowly backed up the stairs and into the kitchen where I kept a bottle of Scotch.

'It's alright,' I told myself as I gulped down a shot. 'I'm only imagining things. It was only a mild hallucination. It's just my fascination with the door. We've been here more than a few months now and it's the only room in the house I don't know intimately. It's the only door I can't get passed, that I can't open, and it's haunting me. It's only my imagination.'

I gulped down another shot of Scotch. Beads of sweat had formed over my brow.

'Christ, I'm sweating.' I thought. 'It must be 20 degrees in here and I'm sweating! My God, the repairman!'

I walked back to the doorway of the kitchen and peered across the foyer to the door to the cellar. I could see the repairman's light.

"Are you alright?"

Nothing.

"I say, would you care for a drink?"

The light did not move. I walked nearer the stairs. Nightmare images filled my mind. I placed one hand against the door frame, my fingers curled over its edge, and slowly peered past the corner.

"Excuse me."

"AHHH!!!!" I screamed. I screamed like a frightened child. Dermot had come up behind me.

"Pardon me. I didn't mean to frighten ya, *again*," he said a little too condescendingly. "I had to go out to my truck and grab the vacuum."

I collected myself.

"Of course. Of course... I *do* apologize. It's just that I fright easily."

"Well, you sure scared me."

"Do you mind if I assist you?" I asked a bit too eagerly.

"Pardon?"

"Well, it's just that I'd like to be of some use. Maybe the work will go faster."

"I suppose you could hold the light. It'll make things easier if I have both hands free."

"It would be my pleasure."

We descended the stairs and I held the light for Dermot. I tried to focus on the light and to not look at the door, but I knew it was there all the same. It was even more frightening to not look at it; to not know what might come out behind me. I just prayed and held the light.

It didn't take long for Dermot to finish the repair. Less than an hour. While he worked on the furnace, he told me about the previous owners and about some of the personal modifications he had done to 'ol Ginny.

He was quite knowledgeable and his father was, in fact, the person responsible for modernizing the furnace to accept natural gas more than 50 years ago. Dermot also maintained the ductwork and heat registers that distributed heat throughout the house.

When he finished, the furnace ignited and once again came to life. The black kettle shape of the furnace, with the ductwork running out the top, and the gaslight glowing through the grate in front, made it appear like some demon billowing heat.

"It will take an hour or so for the house to heat up, but she's done for now. She's a fine machine," Dermot smiled.

"Thank you," I smiled back.

"Well, I like to take care of her. And if I take care of her, she'll take care of you. We'll send you the bill. Oh…"

He handed me something.

"Don't forget your torch."

We ascended the stairs and said our goodbyes. When I closed the front door, I remembered the whisper: "I'm inside."

2

"I'm inside."

I only stayed one night at the house. I kept the bed and my belongings in the upstairs guest room, but I really had no intention of using them unless it was absolutely necessary.

Work on the house continued through the winter. All of the plumbing and electrical systems were removed. Dermot removed all of the old ductwork and began reconditioning the furnace. We were now prepping and repairing the walls and floors to allow for the new systems to go in.

Reconstruction of the roof would begin in the spring as the weather permitted. And all entryways and windows were scheduled for removal and refurbishment. Room by room, and floor by floor, all of the doors and windows would either be refurbished or replaced. I hoped that the structural restoration would be complete before summer.

In January, I decided to enlist the aid of the architectural history department at the University College London to trace the history of the house and to determine how and when the door in the basement came to be sealed. In so doing, I hoped to discover a way of opening it.

I delivered copies of all of the house plans in my possession to Professor Howard Russell, faculty supervisor for the Archive of Architectural History at UCL and Mira Smith, Head of the UCL Library of History. Professor Russell was too busy to assist me personally, but he was kind enough to lend me the aid of one of his research assistants, Agatha Cooper, to help me on site at the house. I was very glad to have her. I also hoped that Ms. Smith would find more than I was able to about the previous owners and occupants of the house.

I never mentioned to anyone those frightful experiences I had over Christmas. They seemed to vanish as mysteriously as they began.

Agatha was a treasure. She was in her late twenties, beautiful and lively, with bright green eyes and deep red hair. Her family was Irish and she was in London pursuing her doctorate in architectural history.

She was more than enthusiastic. She passionately loved architecture and threw herself into her work. She wanted to know and was eager to learn every step of the restoration process.

How we went about to antiquities warehouses and to salvage yards in order to acquire as many period materials as possible. How we cared for and preserved the existing architecture in the process of the restoration, disturbing as little as possible while still fully amending and repairing the structure. How we refurbished old equipment or fabricated parts that we were unable to find, so on and so forth.

I took her through the house, room by room, and explained everything we had done so far. She absorbed everything with immense curiosity. When I took her into the cellar, she was immediately fascinated by the door. Over the next few months she would become obsessed with it.

~

Agatha was tenacious. She went to every city office and excavated literally every set of drawings that were ever produced on the home. A job I thought I had already done, but, to my surprise, she was able to uncover three sets of drawings that I did not know even existed. She was an absolute wonder.

Agatha and I would often stay late into the evening studying the architectural plans and documenting our research. In the weeks we had worked together, we had become friends and enjoyed lengthy conversations over the occasional bottle of wine. She was quite charming and I soon found myself a bit infatuated with her.

As she continued to study the plans for any changes we may have missed, I began cataloguing all of the architectural materials we would need to continue with the restoration. Although we were on a search to detail the exact history of the home, it was still my job and my intention to do as full a restoration as possible, which meant locating and acquiring period moldings, cornices, fixtures, and hardware.

I know it seems rather contradictory, but once the plumbing and electrical systems are replaced with modern equipment, it will become a process of preserving as much of the original, period materials currently in the house as possible and acquiring as much historically accurate period materials as possible to restore the home. It was on one of these evenings that Agatha made a remarkable discovery.

Agatha had a process. She studied every set of drawings of the home in order, beginning with the original plans and ending with the most recent, documenting all of the changes made to the house. By thoroughly studying and documenting all of the changes in each set of drawings, she hoped to uncover when and how the door became sealed. What she actually found was quite different. In fact, it is quite amazing that she stumbled across it at all.

Earlier plans tend to be less sophisticated and concentrate quite heavily on the exterior structure: the foundation, exterior walls, windows, doors, chimneys, and the roof. Very rarely do these early drawings include any significant detail of the interior construction of the house, especially in areas of stairwells, closets, and storage.

We had gone through most of the house physically, systematically, starting in the cellar and working from the front of the house to the back, room by room, and so cross checking every detail we could find with the series of plans we had in our possession.

This home had been renovated more than a dozen times over its 220-year history. Not all major renovations. Sometimes it was just an electrical upgrade or new sewage lines, but, all in all, 6 major renovations and at least as many minor ones.

There were nearly three-dozen sets of drawings that we needed to look through. Not everything can be documented, and in most of the plans, stairwells, closets, and wet walls were simply drawn in as a 'dead space': an area outlined in the plans with no further details given. Generally, it meant that the space was an empty, unused void.

Agatha had discovered a minor discrepancy in two assumingly identical sets of drawings. She was studying the upstairs linen closet when she found a discrepancy in a set of identical plans that were filed at two different offices. This area was continually redrawn as a dead space in every series of drawings that we possessed, save one; and even then it was barely noticeable.

In 1935 a series of small renovations were performed on the house, including increasing the amount of closet space and storage. The set of drawings that were filed with the city commissioner's office, the set that I had, differed ever so slightly from the plans from the city inspector's office, which Agatha had found.

Apparently an opening was cut into the wall of the back guest room to allow access to the space under the attic stairs. It appears in only one drawing as a pair of lines.

The linen closet separates the upstairs large front guest room from the smaller one over the dining room. The linen closet itself is lined with cabinetry, floor to ceiling and nearly wall to wall, with a small staircase leading up to the attic where the servants' quarters were located. The stairwell was quite small and rose in three runs of 5 steps, turning 90 degrees twice, with a landing at each corner as it formed a semicircle leading up to the attic.

In the far back corner of the linen closet, under the staircase and adjoining the back guest room, there was what appeared to be a void in the plans or a dead space; which would have been typical in a Georgian home. Often these small attic staircases were too small to warrant opening the space beneath them.

When we looked at the guest room wall, it appeared to be completely intact. We decided to explore the interior of the linen closet first, believing that there must have been an access panel that was covered by the cabinetry. But the walls inside of the linen closet, behind the cabinets, and under the stairs were all completely intact, leaving the back guest room wall as the only possibility where the opening would be located.

We had already stripped and cleaned all of the walls,

windows, and floors in the back guest room leaving only the dry plaster of the walls and the bare wood of the floors. There were no permutations in the plaster of any kind. We decided to remove the plaster in the area of the dead space to try to locate a seam or break in the wooden structure buried beneath. What we found was a bit of a mystery.

There had been what appeared to be a small closet door within the wall, only instead of merely boarding it up and plastering over it, the opening was purposefully, and carefully removed and a continuation of the existing wall built in its place. It was feathered together so cleanly, that no one under a cursory inspection would ever notice that it was there. It was made, quite purposefully, to disappear. It was a wonder we had even found it at all.

The renovation was not in any of the plans. No other work had been done in that location and in all subsequent plans it was merely drawn in as part of the stairwell. By our accounts, this small closet disappeared almost 100 years ago. When we opened the wall of the back guest room into the closet we had no idea what to expect, but what we did not expect to find was a mausoleum.

We carefully cut into the wall and exposed the closet. It was quite small and filled with woman's clothing. The clothes, or what was left of them, still hung on their hangers. Some were rather well preserved, as if they hadn't aged at all. Others were tattered rags, or worse, a pile of dust on the floor. There were hatboxes and gloves, a small photo album, and some papers.

Opposite the clothing, on a shelf, lay a hickory box. It appeared to be a large portable secretary. The key was still in the lock. At first I didn't want to disturb anything, but I desperately wanted to know what was inside the secretary. I do know I shouldn't have done it, but I was relying on my own expertise and experience in handling and caring for historic artifacts and my curiosity got the better of me.

I took out my kerchief and without touching the secretary with my fingers or moving it from its place on the shelf, I simply lifted the lid and peered inside. I immediately saw the handwritten note resting on top, written in a terrible, almost illegible scrawl. Below it were several journals, and underneath those appeared to be several newspaper clippings and some sort of book. I carefully closed the lid.

"That's amazing," I sighed.

Thomas, my construction manager, the one who successfully opened the wall, spoke next.

"You should call Theresa, at the museum of antiquities, and have her look at all of this. She'll know how to handle it so as not to damage anything," he said.

"You're right. You are so right. I definitely do not want to damage this treasure." And I laughed. "It's a bit like being an archeologist isn't it Tom?"

"Breathtaking. I always love it when we find something. It's like opening one of the pharaoh's tombs."

"I quite agree." And it was, in our own special way.

We often found the odd bits of historic import: a random newspaper clipping or photo; a rare painting or sculpture; sometimes a small box filled with money or jewelry; but never an entire room filled with personal belongings that have not seen the light of day for nearly a century. This was an unbelievable find. I credited Agatha with the discovery. At the time it seemed congratulatory. It would prove to be otherwise.

I knew it would be a number of months for Theresa to go through the findings and document her research, so we continued to finish the structural work and began prepping for the next step, the installation of the new plumbing, electrical systems, and ductwork.

T he next morning I broke the news of the discovery to the team and to the firm. I also told them that we would continue the renovations on the house while Mira, Theresa, and Agatha researched what we had discovered in the hidden closet.

We never found what we were looking for in answer to the door. It still remained sealed. I no longer wanted to know what secrets it held, but I became possessed by an overwhelming urge to open the door. I hired an additional crew of architectural historians to try to find out exactly how and why the door came to be built the way it was. Soon after, something happened. I saw… 'her.'

I remember the exact moment. It was nearing spring and I was at the office sitting at my computer drafting some plans. I looked out my office door, and there she was, holding a drink, talking with a friend. She was dressed all in black, a little veil over her eyes. Not in mourning, God no, it was the fashion; the fashion of the early 20th century.

She was drinking a martini; so somber, so gentle, so confident. She was amazing: sophisticated, intelligent, and elegant. She was beautiful. Just when I thought I could reach out and touch her, she disappeared, and I was staring into the blank space of the common room central to our floor of offices. Nothing but desks and copy machines and the water cooler against the wall. I blinked to make sure this was reality. Then I heard her. 'Come to me,' she said.

It was an apparition yes, but it was so real. She was so real. I could see her image still. Her long black hair cut in a bang across the front. Her narrow dark eyes and supple lips. The way she elegantly held her glass as if it were a tender, fragile thing. Her demeanor, her cantor. I could replay the scene over and again with perfect clarity. I knew she was real. Then I looked at my computer screen and it brought me back to reality. It was an hallucination, nothing more. I was due for a vacation. I decided that after the renovations were finished, I would go on a trip to the French Riviera. I immediately began planning my vacation.

"I have found the perfect woman for you!" Shelly said popping her head into my office.

"Not now, Shelly," I practically begged her.

"Awe, c'mon," she said. "You never go out. You never meet people. I'm just trying to help."

"I know and I appreciate it. I really do. But I'm not the man for that sort of thing. I've never really fancied dating. I much prefer to meet people naturally, through mutual friends and acquaintances."

I could sense her disappointment.

"She's beautiful... and rich!" she said hugging the doorframe seductively.

"My two favorite personality traits. Please Shelly, not tonight."

"I can't. I promised her. She's dying to meet you. I already told her you'd meet her for a drink at Bartleby's at 7:00pm. Got that? Bartleby's 7:00pm. You have to go. She'll be waiting for you."

"You've already promised her, without even asking me? How do you know I'm not previously engaged? Call her and cancel!"

"I can't. She's not at home. She's flying in from Brussels. She lands at 6:00 and I told her you'd meet her at 7:00. And you are *not* previously engaged."

I was really quite perturbed. It was so rude of her to do such a thing and being the gentleman I am, I cannot disappoint someone I am engaged to meet. This really put me in a position.

"Look. You are never going to get married if you don't

start dating," Shelly continued. "Besides, this is just a friendly date. She just wants to get together and have a little 'get to know you' drink. It's harmless." She put on her best pouty face and looked up into my eyes. "I'm just looking out for you," she said. "You know I care about you. I just want to see you happy."

I gave in. What was I to do? I may not be a lot of things, but damn it, I'm honorable. It would be disgraceful to leave a woman sitting at a bar alone on my account. And Shelly was right. I never go out or meet people. I seem to get more reclusive with each passing year. I knew she cared. I couldn't help but to feel grateful.

"You really shouldn't have, Shelly. And I do appreciate it. If it weren't for you I would have no social life at all. But please, next time a little warning."

"No problem."

She hugged me and straightened my tie.

"You look great. Go get her, tiger."

I kissed her on the cheek and went back into my office to gather my things.

∽

I arrived twenty minutes early, checked my coat, asked for a comfortable table with a little privacy, and left a message with the hostess to bring my 'date' to the table when she arrived. I couldn't get the image of the woman from my hallucination out of my head. I sat at the table wondering whether or not I should trust my senses; whether what I saw was real, or if I was losing my sanity. What if all of the things I was experiencing were real. I felt a hand brush against my shoulder and I half expected to see the woman from my hallucination standing there. It nearly was.

"Hi, I'm Amanda, Shelly's friend. Nice to meet you," she said.

"Hello. *Very* nice to meet *you*," I answered.

Amanda was beautiful. A tall, thin, brunette with brown eyes. Smart, confident. I can go on. We had a couple of drinks, talked, and generally had a good time.

"So, you actually had to climb out of the window onto the roof? I thought that only happened in movies," she said laughing a bit.

"Oh yes! My roommate had barred me from going to the political rally. He said it would cause catastrophic harm to my career. 'What career?' I said. 'I'm going into architecture!' 'Precisely!' he yelled, and with the help of some friends he began to pile benches and chairs in front of the door. So, the only way out of my room was to climb out the window and onto the roof of the building. I eventually found my way down and I attended the rally as I had intended."

"My God. University antics," she said and had a sip of her wine.

"You never forget them." I smiled and sipped my brandy.

"So what do you want to do now? You have a successful career. What are your plans?" She leaned in, her head resting on her hands with her elbows propped up on the table.

"Interesting you should ask," I answered, trying to remain humble, but too proud to pull it off. "I just acquired a home. A small Georgian home and I am actually in the process of restoring it to period."

"That's marvelous!" Her eyes glistened with excitement.

"It's been a dream of mine since I was in university," I said.

"I would love to see it," she said rather invitingly. I was

quite flattered, but was a bit self-conscious. I hadn't successfully dated in quite some time. My love had become my work in recent years.

"Well, of course, I would love to show you," I said hoping I didn't sound to nervous. "It's in shambles right now, but you should be able to appreciate where we intend to go with the project. The structural renovations should be complete by late summer."

"That sounds marvelous. We can take a walk by moonlight. Maybe grab a café au lait on the way," she smiled back.

It was quite lovely to have a woman suggest the plans for the evening. She *was* beautiful.

"That would be nice," I smiled back.

Just then, the butterflies in my stomach took flight, and as I was reaching for the check, I spilled her drink, right onto her lap.

"I am so sorry," I said reaching for a napkin.

"No, it's quite alright. What's a little white wine on cashmere? Excuse me, won't you?"

She got up and went to the ladies room. She stopped at the bar along the way and ordered a glass of something. I was completely embarrassed. I get so nervous around woman I am genuinely attracted to. You put me in front of someone I have no interest in at all and I can remain perfectly calm and talk all night. You place a woman I truly desire in front of me and I turn into a clumsy schoolboy.

I always felt like a clumsy schoolboy at these moments. This is usually when my date starts to look at me a little more closely. Seeing me fidget. Watching me as I look down into my plate chewing my food, too bashful to even look her in the eye. Fortunately, we were just having drinks and I had no plate of food to distract me, but I couldn't help blushing and, of course, feeling foolish.

The waitress came by and I paid the check. Amanda took quite a while in the bathroom. Not too long, perhaps. Perhaps, I just thought it took a long while. When she returned, to my surprise, she was smiling.

"Are you ready for that walk?" she asked.

"Why, yes. How's your dress?"

"It's fine. A little club soda and it comes right out. I've been meaning to donate this dress to someone more fitting anyway."

"More fitting."

"I don't usually 'dress up.' I'd rather be more comfortable than fashionable."

I think I fell in love with her at that moment. I didn't think it was possible.

"Where would you like to stop for that café au lait," I asked eagerly.

"We'll follow the moon and see where it leads us," she replied.

"Cheers to *that*," I said.

∽

We had a wonderful evening, Amanda and I. We stopped for coffee and continued our little stroll until it was too chilly to bear. Then we stopped by the home and I showed her everything room by room. Everything except the cellar. I made the excuse that it was too 'dangerous' down there with all of the tools lying about.

I couldn't tell her, of course, but as soon as we entered the house together, I suddenly felt ill at ease and I got the very real sensation that by being here Amanda was in danger. I could feel it, like a tingling sensation up my spine. Something did not want her here. It especially did not want us here together. I tried to ignore it and made the tour as quick as I possibly could without seeming rude. I entered the rooms first and surveyed the corners for any lurking shadows. It was a bit late, so I made the excuse that I needed to get an early start in the morning and called her a cab. We exchanged numbers. We even kissed.

Amanda was a very busy woman. She was only in town for a few days then she would return to Brussels. We made plans to meet again after she returned to England at the end of the summer. As soon as Amanda left, the sensation stopped.

For some reason, I decided to stay the night in the house. It was too late to catch the train to my apartment, but I could have called a cab. Instead I made my way upstairs and got ready for bed. As soon as I was in bed, I quickly forgot about the sensation I felt earlier and fell into a deep slumber. That night I had a marvelous dream. I dreamt of a beautiful woman.

"Come to me," she said and she beckoned me to come closer. "I'm waiting for you."

I could see her lips, so soft and round and glistening. She called me forward, curling her index finger in a gesture that tugged at my very heart, leading me into bed. Her beautiful, long, black hair fell past her shoulders, her bangs cut straight across, above her eyes. Hey eyebrows peaked in a sharp crescent then ending in a gentle swoop. And her eyes a very deep green. So beautiful. So perfect.

I felt the softness of her hair and brushed her cheek. She danced playfully and sashayed her hips. And I loved her. She was everything I ever imagined in a woman. She was perfect. I wanted so desperately to be with her, but I was restrained. I could not move closer to her, something was forbidding it. I could feel her breath on my skin as she spoke, but I couldn't understand her words. It was beautiful. It was torture. Then I woke up.

3

"Come to me."

Our firm possessed an extensive library, a large section of which was devoted to architectural history, and of course, I had my own private library. Between the two and with some help from my friends at the public library, Mira and I were able to gain a rather good understanding of the history of the home, as far as ownership was concerned.

The flagstone on the house read 1787, so we started there. Apparently, the house was originally commissioned by a Lord Walter Bennington as a gift for the son of his favorite sister Gwendaline Bennington Rutherford. This young nephew, one Arthur Rutherford II, died rather unfortunately in 1817. The home remained in the Rutherford family until 1835, at which time it was passed onto a General Henry Taft, who lived there until his death in March 1892.

The home was held in trust until September 1894 when it was purchased by a Mr. Frederick Duvall for his wife Mildred "Millie" Duvall. He, apparently, kept a separate residence in France in order to remain close to his businesses and other assets. He and Mildred had one son named Charles, born in May 1908. Frederick Duvall died in August 1928 and left the sum of his fortune to Mildred. Mildred died in April 1930 and left the home and her wealth in trust for young Charles. In May 1933, Charles claimed his inheritance and in April 1935, Charles married one Elizabeth Colt. The following year they had one child, a daughter named Allison, who died after only 18 months. In January 1938, Elizabeth joined the missionary and left for East India. Elizabeth disappeared from record. Charles continued to live in the house until his death in 1939.

Charles' eldest cousin Edward Grant inherited the house and held it in trust until 1940, when Edward offered the home to the Oddfellows as an emergency triage during the bombing of London. The home has been operating under their auspices ever since. That is, until recent economic struggles made it difficult for them to afford the general upkeep of the property. So, the home was put up for auction, at which time it was purchased by Randall and Sons, whom we acquired the property from a few months later.

Based on these records, the home was under the ownership of Charles Duvall and Elizabeth Colt Duvall when the closet both appeared and disappeared.

∽

As spring arrived, Agatha had become obsessed with our find. She researched and catalogued everything we had pulled from the closet with Theresa. She contacted

Mira to see what she had found out about the life and history of the families who lived in the home. She catalogued, and researched, and wrote almost continually without stop. She was absolutely determined to find out exactly what had happened in that home. She wasn't the same as she was when she found the discrepancy in the plans. She was driven by something much more powerful. She seemed desperate, almost frantic, to find the answers. She stopped by the office to share her recent findings with me.

"Something very terrible happened in that house, Andrew," Agatha confided in me.

"What do you mean?" I asked.

"We've been trying to have what was written in the journals translated. There are passages, entire pages, in fact, written in ancient Babylonian and Sumerian. With several references to the occult." She put her hand on mine and pleaded with me with her eyes to believe her.

"The occult?" I asked back rather timidly. Black swirls and mist filled my imagination. Then the blackened façade of the door slammed into focus.

"We disturbed… something… when we found the closet in the upstairs bedroom. It was sleeping… and it blames me for waking it, because I'm the one who found it." Her hand gripped my hand very tightly. So tightly it was painful.

I paused to look at her. The poor girl was fidgeting. She had chewed her fingernails to the cuticles. Her hair was unkempt. Her legs bounced.

"Agatha, what you're saying doesn't make any sense." I tried to gently pull my hand from hers by placing my other hand on top and stroking her hand gently, but she would not let go.

"Whatever it is, it can't leave the house. It is trapped

inside the house. It wants to hurt me, Andrew. I'm having nightmares. I can't sleep. It's haunting me."

Her eyes looked glazed over, but filled with a very palpable fear. I finally managed to pull my hand free. And I placed her hand onto her lap.

"What do you mean… it?" I asked very deliberately.

"It's behind the door… in the cellar. It's trapped by the door." She grabbed my hand again with both of hers. Her fingers dug into my hand painfully. "Promise me you will never open that door."

A shiver ran down my spine. 'Come to me. I'm inside,' the apparition with green eyes said to me just nights before.

"It's not human Andrew. It's something else." She fidgeted in her chair. Her eyes pleaded with me.

"I don't under…" I started.

"Don't tell me you don't understand!" she yelled.

I had to get up and shut my office door so that no one panicked and called the police. I tried to calm her down.

"Ok. Maybe I do understand. A bit. But, I don't see what harm…"

"Don't say that. You don't know what this thing has been doing to me. It's torturing me. It's making me feel what it feels. Andrew, you do not want to help this thing. Believe me, you don't."

Suddenly, Agatha's eyes darted as if she saw something behind me. She clenched her fists in fright. Sheer panic filled her eyes. I turned around and saw nothing.

"What is it, Agatha?" I asked perplexed and a bit worried.

"It knows I'm here. It knows I told you." She handed me a manila envelope. "Take these." I took the envelope. "They're translations of the journals and photographs of all of the previous owners. Read them, Andrew."

I started to ask if she needed help, uncertain of her condition, but she stopped me.

"If you don't believe me, go see Theresa. She still has the originals." Her eyes darted to the corner of the room again. "I have to go Andrew." She got up hurriedly and headed for the door. She turned back for just a moment. "Never open that door," she said and then she left.

As she walked away I noticed how badly her clothes were wrinkled. She looked as if she hadn't slept in weeks. I thought to call an ambulance for her. She seemed like she were having a nervous breakdown. In the end, I just held onto the manila envelope she gave me and watched her leave.

∼

I know that Agatha gave me copies, but I had to see Theresa. I had to read the originals. Theresa was a good friend. One of the curators at the British National Museum of Antiquities, she specialized in British artifacts dating from the early 17th century through the late 20th century. She knew nearly all there was to know about the type of artifacts we found in that closet and I was glad to have her as the one to curate and catalogue the discovery. I knew that she would allow me certain privileges that other curators would not, such as allowing me to personally peruse the artifacts.

We were old college chums, she and I, and well, those ties of friendship and loyalty are often built by having done things we shouldn't have and having kept each other out of trouble. Which meant we owed each other and we both knew how to keep a secret. I went to visit Theresa to see what she had discovered, but secretly, I hoped to have a closer look at what was in that secretary.

∼

"Y̲ou're not going to believe what you've found!" Theresa was both excited and a bit withdrawn.

"Is it good?"

"The artifacts themselves are more than good. They're simply... they're simply marvelous. Some of these items must have been in the family for generations. According to your documents the home was built in 1787. Some of these artifacts predate that. Others are most probably from somewhere between 1850 and 1880. The latest articles are from the mid to late 1930's. Definitely from the genteel class, although I did find an odd collection of woman's bath and hair accessories that were clearly from the working class.

"It is a rare collection of items. And It will take some time to establish provenance, but several of these items are extremely valuable and from an obviously wealthy family."

"Well, I am so glad that you are happy. Did you find anything... peculiar? Anything of special importance? That might also help me in the restoration or in better knowing the history of the home?" I watched her face as I asked. Her expression changed.

"Funny you should ask. Do you know something I don't?" She crossed over to a table where all of the journals were catalogued and stored.

"I just thought... the way that it was hidden. I mean purposefully hidden, there must be some secret hidden within all of those belongings. Isn't there?" I hoped I didn't seem too anxious when I asked.

"You've no idea what you've found do you?" She lifted a brown leather journal from the table, turned to a page, and showed it to me. "Apparently, whoever owned these items practiced some sort of black magic or occult rituals."

The page she showed me was covered in ancient Babylonian symbols, occult symbols, and words written in what appeared to be Latin.

"We've made copies and are having them translated," she said. "Look at the bottom of the page."

I looked and there were several dark stains on the bottom portion of the page.

"What is it?" I asked

"Blood," she said. "We had some people from forensic science analyze it. It's human."

"Human?" I held the book away from me and looked at the stains in the light.

"Those pages document a spell or a ritual that they performed requiring the blood of a victim to be drunk," she continued. "We think perhaps they spilled some of it while they were reciting from the book. We're still uncovering more as more pages are translated, but what we have discovered so far is quite unsettling.

"The journals are dated so we are having the pages translated chronologically. Not all of the pages are in ancient languages. Most of them are written in English. But what is written in the ancient languages seem to be periodic dispersals of spells, rituals, and... events."

"What do you mean... events?" I flipped through more pages of the journal.

"Whoever wrote these journals wrote them as a kind of diary cataloguing some of the things they'd done at those rituals... to people. To people they murdered."

"Murdered?" I closed the book and set it back on the table.

"It's gruesome, I know, but what we've uncovered so far is that these events, in fact, everything that is recorded in these journals are all interconnected and they seem to have all been performed for a single purpose."

"What purpose?" I asked.

"The resurrection of an ancient Babylonian demon," she answered.

∼

I returned to the home that evening, the manila envelope that Agatha gave me in hand. I hung my coat in the foyer walked straight into the kitchen and poured myself a Scotch. I sat in the kitchen, drink in hand, and went over the plans for the house in my head.

It was mid-April now. All of the plumbing and electrical systems were in. The furnace had been restored and the new ductwork put in. All of the walls were plastered. All of the interior doors had been removed for stripping and reconditioning. Several of the upstairs windows had been removed for the same reason. And reconstruction of the roof was well underway.

I had a meeting with the interior designer in the morning to plan the wall and window treatments, furnishings, and the decorations. Such a wonderful home I thought... with such a horrible history. I drank the Scotch in one gulp and poured another.

After I'd had one too many, I grabbed the bottle and stumbled through the foyer to the top of the stairs leading to the cellar. It was dusk, but we had electricity now. I tried the light switch. No light came on. I tried again. Nothing. I looked into the cool darkness of the cellar. 'Demons,' I thought.

My head began to pound. I had to close my eyes and steady myself by leaning against the doorframe. I could feel each heartbeat pounding in my head. I don't know how long I had been standing there, or when I first heard it, but music drifted into my senses. I felt it before I heard it, and it filled my mind. Jazz music. 1920's jazz music:

"Pack up all my care and woe, here I go, singing low,

Bye bye blackbird. Where somebody waits for me, sugar's sweet, so is she, bye bye blackbird."

I opened my eyes and as things slowly came into focus, I noticed a glow at the bottom of the stairs. A soft pink and purple light shone in the darkness. The music filled my ears, and then, the sound of her laugh: playful, gentle, inviting; beckoning me forward. I listened and I descended the stairs.

I followed the light to its source. It was coming from the keyhole in the door. I tried to look through the keyhole, but the light was too bright. I put my ear against the door. I could hear the music coming from inside. I closed my eyes. Swirls of smoke filled my mind, and through the smoke, a shape, engulfed in pink and purple ethereal light. I strained until the shape came into focus, and there she was. So beautiful. So perfect. Wearing black lingerie, lying on a chaise lounge her hand in the air swaying to the rhythm of the music. I lowered myself to the floor and listened.

I awoke in the morning. I was sitting on the floor, leaning against the door. The empty Scotch bottle lay next to me. The door was cold and hard. I turned my head to look at it. I ran my fingers down its black surface.

"Demons don't exist," I said.

I stood up and went upstairs to change clothes.

∼

I dressed and got ready for my meeting with the interior designer. I walked through the foyer on the way to the study where I planned to hold our meeting, but as I approached the door, I became drawn to the parlor and walked in there instead.

The morning sun shone through the windows. It felt warm. I walked over to the fireplace and inspected the mantle. It needed a clock. A brass clock with a smooth curving surface and white face with roman numerals. I took a step back from the fireplace and looked around the room. The room needed vertically striped wallpaper; yellow and pink. Not bright and gaudy, but subtle, like pastels. With a chaise lounge placed on an oriental rug in front of the fireplace.

I closed my eyes and envisioned the room. Dark hardwood floors. A curio cabinet in the corner on the wall opposite the fireplace. A divan under the front windows. A low table in front of it. The color and style of the furnishings were vintage from the 1920's and 30's.

I opened my eyes. I could see the entire room completely furnished. I closed my eyes and imagined each room of the house. I could see the tables and chairs. The cabinets. The paintings. The decorations. Even the crystal doorknobs.

I walked from room to room and in my mind and imagination I could see exactly how each room was furnished and decorated. I could see how I wanted everything to be. They way they needed to be. I started writing it down as I went from room to room.

I walked into the study. The makeshift table had been replaced with a proper desk in front of the windows. The manila envelope lay on top of it. I didn't remember putting it there. I sat at the desk, opened the envelope and took out the contents.

Agatha may have been a wreck when I last saw her, but the contents of the envelope were meticulously organized. The first few pages were a brief history of all of the previous owners of the home including the Duvall family both before Mr. and Mrs. Duvall passed and after they had and left the home to their son Charles.

There was a brief history of Charles Duvall and Elizabeth Colt along with a brief account of their daughter, Allison; a chronological translation of the rituals and events that took place in the house; and a series of photographs of all of the known occupants of the home, including a photograph of the entire Duvall household and the servants.

On each of the photographs of the men who owned the home, Agatha had drawn the symbol of the 'All-Seeing Eye.' An Egyptian symbol often used by the Illuminati; which is purported to be a secret society of the world's wealthiest individuals and families. Was Agatha saying that all of these men were members of the Illuminati? I started reading.

I began with the written chronological history of the persons who had previously owned the home and I compared them with their photographs. Above the heads of each of the men in the families, Agatha had drawn the symbol for the all-seeing eye. And within the chronology she included a diagram of a family tree. It appears all of the previous owners, including some members in the Oddfellows, were all related; first and second cousins... and their families intermarried to keep the house within their possession.

It made me wonder why the house was sold in the first place. If the home had remained in the family the entire time, why did they sell it now? They all seemed to be wealthy. None of them would have had any problems affording the upkeep of the house as the Oddfellows had claimed. Maybe they just wanted to be rid of it. But the home was pristine. There must be some other reason why they chose to sell it.

I looked through more of the papers, and found the information about the rituals and events that took place in the home. According to Mira and Theresa the incantations dated back to the late Sumerian civilization and the ancient city of Babylon around 2200 BC. They said that the most common days for these rituals to be performed were during the summer and winter solstices; that these rituals could only be performed during the proper alignments of certain planets, the moon, and other constellations; and that these alignments could only be predicted by those who possessed a profound understanding of an ancient Babylonian mathematics known only to those who practiced occult demonology.

Apparently, all of the rituals were performed in an effort to resurrect a specific Babylonian demon or god who would… 'bring about the end of the world.' And this 'end' would be a cleansing of the earth that would usher in a new age of enlightenment where evil would rule the world.

According to Agatha's notes, all of the families who lived in the house practiced the same Babylonian occult religion for the sole purpose of resurrecting this ancient Babylonian demon. They performed all of the rituals in a single location that was believed to be the location of two intersecting ley lines. And the rituals were performed in that location for more than 200 years.

Agatha included an arial photograph of the house and its surrounding properties and a diagram with the locations of several intersecting ley lines throughout the world. One pair of which lay directly underneath the property that this house was built on. According to Agatha, hundreds of these rituals were performed at this location. And the exact location where these ritual were performed was in the room blocked by that black door in the cellar.

She went on to translate some of the events that occurred at these rituals. During one ritual, a man was bound by wire and his ears, tongue, and eyes were removed to keep this man deaf, silent, and blind, so that no one would ever discover who they were or what they were doing. 'To keep their ways secret,' it said. Another went on to describe how a pregnant woman in her third trimester was ritually murdered to remove her uterus while the unborn infant was still inside and then the womb was placed into a fire and burned, killing the child while it was still in the womb. And they did this in order to gain the power to destroy life from its beginnings, from its origins.

Agatha translated more than thirty of these passages taken from the journal. Each one more gruesome and horrifying than the last. No wonder she was so distraught.

I looked at my hand, it was shaking. I put the papers down and went straight into the kitchen to pour myself a drink. I needed to calm my nerves. I closed my eyes and saw images of what was done to those people during those rituals. But it wasn't just in my mind or my imagination. It was as if I were actually watching them as they happened.

People wearing purple robes with hoods over their heads stood in a circle. Priests in purple robes with purple and white vestments recited incantations. Gold and Silver candelabras lit the room. And the image of Baphomet within an inverted pentagram was painted on the wall. Along with the all-seeing eye. Everyone in the room chanted phrases in unison in some unknown and ancient language.

I poured myself another drink. My hands were still shaking. I could hear them chanting in my head. I could hear them, but I couldn't understand what they were saying. The words came out as a rhythmic hum of noise that was barely audible at first. Then it grew louder and faster… Eso To Gat Ether Hume… Eso To Gat Ether Hume… Eso To Gat Ether Hume… BOOM! BOOM! BOOM! The iron ring on the door in the cellar shook. Something was pounding on the door.

"Andrew?"

Rebecca, the interior designer, had come up behind me. I tried to compose myself.

"Hello Rebecca," I said. "Forgive me I'm having a moment of frustration."

Rebecca looked at the empty tumbler in my hand.

"And it's driving you to drink?" she laughed. "Well, did you come back to your senses? Can we get to work?"

"Of course."

We walked to my desk in the study. I quickly gathered up all of the papers Agatha had given me and put them back into the Manila envelope. I opened the desk drawer and put the envelop inside and out of sight.

"I have a very good idea of how I would like to furnish and decorate the home," I said, finally regaining my senses. "I even wrote a lot of it down. But once I saw the bare floors, I knew I was in over my head acquiring anything, so, I hoped that you could come rescue me."

"Why didn't you call me earlier?" Rebecca removed a yellow legal pad and a pen from her briefcase. "We could have been half way finished by now."

"I didn't really know what direction I wanted to take until recently. I'm thinking vintage 1920's and 30's."

"Well that sounds interesting. I like it, but why do you want it?"

"Hmmm… well, I don't know." I thought about the odd moment of inspiration I had earlier that morning. "A lot of it I wrote down just this morning before you arrived. A moment of inspiration you could say." I handed Rebecca my notes. "I wanted to do it myself and then I realized that even though I know every shop where I can find hardware and moldings, I haven't a clue where to find the furnishings."

"Is this your home now?" Rebecca paused from taking her notes. "You're furnishing it yourself."

"The paperwork isn't done yet, but yes, hopefully by the end of the year the paperwork will be filed and I will be the proud new owner of the property."

"Oh my God! Congratulations." Rebecca stood up and gave me a hug. "Do you mind if we get started right away? I'd like to have a look around."

"No, not at all. You can leave your things in the study."

Rebecca removed a camera from her pocket.

"Where do you want to start?" she said as she checked the settings on her camera.

"In the parlor, I suppose."

I led her through the foyer and into the parlor. She began photographing every detail of the room.

"I was thinking that we could use some pink and yellow vertically striped wallpaper in here, on the upper half of the walls, and a whitewashed wainscoting underneath," I said.

"Is that your idea?"

"Yes. I'm afraid it is."

"Oh, it's not bad," she said. "More feminine than I would have thought. What else did you have in mind?"

"Oh, a chaise lounge in front of the fireplace. With an oriental rug underneath."

"I like where your head is at, Andrew. This should be fun."

As we walked through the house, Rebecca asked me questions. I answered them. And before long we had managed to tour most of the home. We had settled on a French Kitchen and Italian baths.

"What about the tub?" she said. "Built in or free standing? Modern or classic. We could put in a spa tub, if you like."

Suddenly, I felt something directing my thoughts. Not

commanding me or telling me what to do, but leading me around the room showing me. I felt as if I were being directed by a partner or a mutual friend.

"Uh, no," I said. "Freestanding porcelain four pedestal tub. Oval."

"The ones with the lion's feet, as they call them?" Rebecca asked.

"That's the one."

"High back or low?"

"High," I said and I could hear the words in my mind before I said them. "It should have a long elegant swoop. Like a dove's wing."

"Dove's wing?" she replied a bit amused. "I think I know which kind you are describing. And the sink?"

Again the tugging within my mind directing me to that side of the room.

"Freestanding white porcelain sink with an oval shaving mirror above it."

"Hmmm... I like how specific you are being. To be honest the more details I have the easier my job becomes. I can just go straight to what you want."

"I hope I'm not a burden."

"Andrew, how long have we worked together?"

"Well over ten years, I suppose."

"And how often have we fought."

"Never. That I can remember."

"You're the client," she said. "It's my job to make you happy. Whether I think it's hideous or not is not important. It's your home. It's your decision. And I will do everything I can to get it right."

"I appreciate that, as always," I said.

We worked our way through the house and back to the study.

"Now the big question," she said. "I am assuming that you want all period materials. Reupholstered, of course."

"Yes. All period furnishings," I said.

"That is not easy to do. And it gets quite expensive."

"I can only imagine."

"I don't want to get into a bidding war over an item you want, Andrew. Some things we'll be able to get quite easily. Some we won't or not at all. You'll have to be accommodating."

"Yes. Of course. I know how it goes," I said. "I had a time locating all of the French hardware for the doors. I couldn't find enough. So, I used Dutch on the smaller doors and closets."

"Then we should be able to agree on most things and this will be a pleasure."

"Oh. There is one thing that must be absolutely perfect."

"Oh, you don't know how much I dread hearing those words, Andrew," she said. "Well, which item is it?"

I could hear her voice in my ear, telling me what to say.

"The chaise lounge in the parlor. It's a very particular French chaise lounge from the early 1920s."

"I'll do some research. I'll show you photos. And when you see it you tell me which one it is. If I can find it, I will get it."

"And the upholstery to match," I said without thinking.

"Period upholstery?" she said.

"Yes. Red velvet upholstery. With a mahogany frame. Art Nouveau."

"That is a very classic style. I'm not sure if upholstery that old will withstand the test of time, Andrew. Even if we do find it."

"Just do your best, I suppose."

When we finished, Rebecca pulled on her long black gloves, and put on her jacket. We said our goodbyes and she left.

As soon as she was gone, I grabbed my coat and ran

from the house. My mind was still filled with images of torture and rape... mutilation... and... human sacrifice. I made my way to the river and leaned against the railing trying to clear my mind. I looked up at the sky. It was a cloudy spring morning. 'Make it stop,' I thought. The images began to spin and swirl within my mind. 'Make it stop. Make it stop. Please make it stop!'

'Shhh!' I heard her in my head, the woman on the chaise lounge, softly whispering in my ear, calming me, soothing me. 'Let me out,' she whispered.

4

"Let Me Out."

Work on the interior of the house continued right on schedule over the next few months. By late summer, all of the windows and doors had been finished and reinstalled all of the walls on both the upper and lower floors had been painted. And all of the floors had been refinished. The Kitchen and guest bathroom were completely finished and most of the rooms were furnished.

The roofing crews started in late April. It took some time to find enough period lumber to repair the roof. But once we had it, within a few weeks they had rebuilt the entire southwest corner and had begun putting the new roofing tiles on.

Rebecca checked in periodically to show me pictures of items she found: beds, dressers, tables and chairs. The ones I liked we went to look at. And if the price was reasonable, we purchased them and had them delivered to the house.

One by one we began acquiring all of the furniture and decorations.

With everything on the house going so well, I turned my attention to the carriage house. Structurally, it was quite sound. It only needed a face lift. The general stripping and cleaning had already been done. After the roofing crew was finished with the house, they moved on to the carriage house. The roof of the carriage house was almost finished.

The drive leading to the road was a very nice crushed brown gravel that matched the path in the front courtyard. I decided to keep it. But the floor of the carriage house seemed to be covered with remnant blocks of concrete salvaged from somewhere else and pieced together in a very poorly planned mosaic. I decided that it had to go, so crews had come in to remove the old pieces of concrete and prep the floor for a new covering of cobblestone.

A large dumpster had already been dropped off and was sitting in the drive. The crew began to break apart the concrete with jackhammers and load it all into the dumpster. I watched them work for a bit and was about to go back into the house when one of the contractors stopped me.

"Excuse me, sir. Mr. Martin," he said. "I think you need to call the police."

"The police?" I said. "Why on earth…"

But he interrupted me.

"Could you just come with me sir. And have a look."

I walked towards the carriage house. All of the workers had stopped and were leaving.

"Are they on break?" I asked.

"If you could just come with me, sir."

The contractor lead me into the carriage house. A large section of the broken concrete had been removed and they seemed to have found something underneath it.

"If you could sir, just have a look, but don't touch it," he said and he lowered himself to the ground. "It's right here sir." He motioned to a shape lying in the dirt that was found underneath the concrete. "We think it's a body."

"A body?"

"Yes sir," he continued. "This shape here appears to be a body wrapped in a canvas bag or blanket of some sort. I think we should call the police to have a look at it."

Very clearly within the dirt I could see the outline of a human shape wrapped in canvas. Images of the rituals swirled within my head. I pinched my nose and tried to concentrate.

"We'll be stopping for the day, sir," the contractor said. "Until we can clear this up."

"Yes, of course," I said. "Well, I'll call you when this has been resolved then."

"Much obliged, sir. We'll still finish the job once it's been removed and the police say that we're clear to proceed."

"Yes. Of course. Thank you." I stood looking at the body. I looked around and noticed that all of the crews had stopped. 'Good news travels fast,' I thought.

"Right. Everyone stop!" I shouted. "I'll need to speak with all of the construction managers in my office in 15 minutes please. Thank you."

All of the crews stopped working and began to pack their things. This was disastrous. This could hold up the project for weeks if not longer. Not to mention what the firm might say about it, company reputation and all. They'll want to hush it up before word gets out. Oh, I imagine it's not the first work crew that has stumbled across the remains of the deceased, but it's the first time it's ever happened on one of my projects. And at my new home of all places.

I thought of all of the rituals that were written about

in those journals that Agatha had translated and left for me to read. Her state of mind began to make more and more sense to me. I decided I should call her later that evening. The discovery of the body might upset her even more, but she knew more about this than I'd bothered to listen to her about. I thought about how rudely I dismissed what she had tried to warn me of. She had to know more. I needed to find out what else she uncovered, face to face.

The crews all stopped and went home. I called the office and informed our lawyers of the morning's events. They advised me not to say anything to the police without the consultation of our lawyers or without a lawyer being present. And they immediately put out a gag order preventing anyone from speaking about the morning's events. They said they would handle it.

A lawyer at the firm called the police and had them sent over. I went into the study and removed the manilla envelope that Agatha had given me from the desk. I didn't know what to do with it, so, I buried it in the bottom of my briefcase. I called all of the construction managers into the study and informed them that we would be suspending any further construction or renovations to the home until the completion of the investigation. Then I informed them of the gag order the firm was issuing to prevent the news from traveling too far and asked them to inform their crews to keep a lid on it.

After that, I simply waited for the police to arrive and when they did, I directed them to the carriage house and left them alone. One officer tried to ask me a few questions, but I simply told him that I would need to consult my lawyer before doing so. He didn't seem to take like that, but he didn't put up a fuss about it either. Some of the police officers tried to question the workers, but most kept their mouths shut and went home. After an hour or so, one of our company lawyers knocked on the front door. I let him in and we went into the study.

~

"Hello. Andrew isn't it?" he said putting out his hand. I shook it. "My name is Stephen George." He was younger than I thought he'd be. In his mid-thirties perhaps. "So, what's all this about?"

"Would you care for a drink?" I said.

"No. Not for me. Thank you."

"Do you mind if I do?"

"No. Not at all."

"Good. Because I need one." I poured myself a brandy and sat at my desk. "It's a beautiful home isn't it?"

"It seems to be." Mr. George looked like a schoolboy with a wry grin on his face. "I'm concerned about what they found this morning."

"You and I both. This could hold us up for months."

I finished my brandy and poured another. Mr. George didn't seem to mind.

"Months? Why so long?"

"Because of complications," I said. "This wonderful home keeps producing one mystery after another. First, we have a door that we cannot open without destroying it. Then, we find a hidden closet in one of the upstairs bedrooms filled with artifacts, some well over one hundred years old. And now, we have a dead body on the premises."

"I heard about the hidden closet." Mr. George's curiosity seemed to be peaked. He leaned forward in his chair. "It's the reason why I asked to be assigned to this case. And the door in the cellar. It's like a murder mystery on television."

I laughed.

"Well, I'm not one to spread gossip, but some items

were found in this house that seem to detail some pretty grim events that may have taken place on this property."

"Such as?" The wry grin on his face widened.

"Well, murder, for one," I said. "That body might not be the only one on the premises."

"There may be more?"

"Possibly. In that room in the cellar, with the door we haven't been able to breach yet."

"Oh, I see," he said. "And the inspectors might want to search the property."

"Exactly," I said. "One body has already been found and that is more than enough for us to deal with, but with this room in the cellar that we have not been able to get into and have no way of knowing what is inside…"

"It could complicate things."

Mr. George finally got the hint.

"Yes. Very much so. I would have no problem allowing the police to enter and to inspect that room in the cellar, if we could open the door without destroying it. My job is historic restoration and preservation and I would like for that door to remain intact and to preserve its architectural integrity and its history."

"I see. But if the police know about it, they might get a court order to breach it without preserving its architectural and historic significance."

"Precisely," I said. "And that, we cannot allow them to do."

"Bully."

"Righto."

"I think we can prevent them from searching the premises," he said. "We can stymy them in litigation until we, ourselves, have an opportunity to open the door while keeping it intact."

"I would be ever so grateful." I leaned back in my chair.

"If you don't mind my asking, what did you find in the upstairs closet?" he said.

"I'm not sure if I'm the one to tell you," I said. "Those findings are being held in the strictest confidence. Only the research team at UCL is privy to that information."

"But you found it. You must know something."

"Well, technically, a research assistant found it. She is the one credited with its discovery, not I."

"A woman found it?"

He seemed thrown off. I tried to assess what he was getting at.

"Man, woman. What's it matter?"

"Patronage," he said rather matter of factly. "Patronage is usually afforded to the men. Not so often to a woman."

"Whose patronage?" I said.

"I just assumed it was you that discovered it is all," he said. "You being a man."

"Well, it was a woman who found it and it was a woman's closet that she found." I said too much. The brandy must have made me more liberal minded than I thought. I needed to bury this before I got long winded.

"A woman's closet?" he said.

"With mostly women's artifacts inside, yes. Like I said, I'm not sure if I am the person to be talking about this. You really should direct your questions to the research team at UCL. They are the ones who know all of the details. I was merely there when we opened it up. I still haven't seen any of it myself."

"Oh, I see. And the research assistant who found it. What was her name?"

I paused a moment. He was getting awfully chatty. Why did he want to know so much? I put down my drink.

"Is there anything else you need in order to block the police from inspecting the cellar?" I said.

"Well yes," he said. "All of your records about the attempts you've made to breach the door while preserving it. And details about the door itself and why it is such an important historic artifact. We will have to build a case around its historic significance to the home in order to argue that it has an intrinsic value that must be preserved."

"I have all of that paperwork at the office. Just let me know where to send it."

"Of course. If you could fax me the documents it would be very helpful." He handed me a card. "That's my office fax number at the bottom."

"I'll do it first thing tomorrow morning," I said and stood up to walk him out.

"Oh yes." He started to put his things away then stopped. "Before I go, would you mind terribly, if I had a look at the door? Possibly take a photo or two with my camera?"

"No. Not at all. Follow me."

I lead the inquisitive Mr. Stephen George down into the cellar. I turned on the light so that we could see the door better. The young Mr. George ran straight to it, took out his camera, and began taking photographs.

"Marvelous," he said. "It's so black."

"Coal soot," I said. "From years of having a coal furnace before it was converted to gas."

"It looks absolutely massive."

"I know. I said the same thing when I first saw it."

Mr. George's eyes seemed to bulge out of his head he was staring at the door so intensely. At one point he rubbed his hand along its surface and it sounded like he mumbled something.

"Can I see it with the light off?"

"With the light off?" I said.

"I want to see what it looks like under natural light."

I turned the lights off. The room dimmed but it was

barely past noon so there was plenty of light to see. I watched the young Mr. George take photo after photo. The pull ring. The lock. The metal bands. The stone archway. He catalogued every detail.

"What do you think is on the other side?" he said.

I looked at the door... blackened with soot... dust drifting through the air. I remembered some of the passages I read that Agatha had translated. And a knot formed in my stomach. Mr. George looked like a fashion photographer obsessed with a pretty model, taking photo after photo of the door.

My heart began to pound and my head began to throb. I could feel the blood pressure building in my temples as each thud pounded in my chest. In my mind, I began to hear glasses clinking as people made a toast with champagne. I saw images of people at a dinner party... carving up and eating meat. I almost blacked out.

"Mr. Martin," the young Mr. George said. "Are you alright?"

I realized that I was leaning against the wall and Mr. George was helping to hold me up.

"My God. Did I almost faint?"

"I believe you did."

"Too much excitement for one day, I suppose," I said.

"I suppose so," he answered. "Should we go back up?"

"Yes. And thank you"

"No problem at all," he said. "These photos will help us prove our case."

"That's good."

Both of us ascended the stairs back into the sunlight and walked back into the study.

"Well, I'll get started on the paperwork to block their inspection of the interior of the home until they obtain a warrant." Mr. George busied himself with putting away his camera and notes. "We'll try to keep them outside the walls first and see how well we do.

"If they can prove cause, they might find a sympathetic judge who will sign a warrant allowing them to search the house. And if they find out there is a room that even we have not been able to properly inspect, they might have enough leverage to ask that the door be removed.

"But, because I am sure that we can find witnesses to attest that the door has not been opened in decades, it would not be urgent for them to breach the door, as there is no active case requiring them to do so. It would be solely for the benefit of the family members who might want to know whose body was found in the carriage house or other persons familiar with the house with missing loved ones.

"All in all, I don't think we'll have anything to worry about. I might even know a person or two who might be able to help you get through that lock. I'll call you in a week or so to take a deposition."

"Thank you very much for your help," I said.

"Not at all," he said. "Wait for my phone call. Oh, we've issued a gag order. I will deliver it to the chief inspector outside. Please tell no one of what they've found."

"Right. Of course."

"Not even your research team at UCL. One last thing, it should only take a moment. I will need you to speak with the chief inspector outside. But, only give him your name and possibly describe your position at the firm and nothing more. No details about the house, its reconstruction, or the door in the cellar."

"That's fine with me," I said. "I'd rather keep my nose out of it."

"That would be best," he said. "From now on you only talk to me. If the police call you, do not answer any of their questions unless I am present."

∽

Mr. George and I walked through the yard to the carriage house. The police had put up yellow tape closing off the carriage house and two or three people were slowly and carefully unearthing the body like they were excavating a mummy from some lost tomb. They had opened the canvas and exposed the head and shoulders. The remains were mostly bone. I noticed a large hole in the right side of the skull before an officer asked me to step back.

"Which of you is the chief inspector?" Mr. George said.

"I am," said a man in a grey suit waving his hand in the air.

"I am Mr. George. I represent the firm that owns the property... and this is Mr. Andrew Martin. He is leading the restoration of the home and its property. If you have any questions for Mr. Martin, please direct them to my office. Here is my card."

Mr. George handed the chief inspector his business card. Then he handed the chief inspector some paperwork.

"And here is a gag order issued by our firm directing you not to speak of your findings to anyone not pertinent to the case, including the press."

"We'd like to search the rest of the premises," the chief inspector said.

"And we'd be happy to oblige as soon as you prove cause to do so," answered Mr. George.

"You want us to get a warrant to inspect the house?" said the chief inspector.

"We see no immediate reason why you would need to investigate any further, including inspecting the interior of

72

the home," said Mr. George. "Please contact our office if you require anything further. Good day."

"Just one moment," the chief inspector said. "Who found the body?"

Mr. George nodded in my direction.

"One of the construction workers contracted to remove and replace the floor in the carriage house. I have their number inside," I said.

"We'd like to speak with them," said the chief inspector.

Mr. George stepped in once again.

"Call my office and we will be happy to provide you with their contact information and any other details you might need."

The chief inspector just waved the paperwork in the air.

"I suppose that's all then," said the chief inspector. "We'll be in touch. Mr. Martin, is it? Don't leave the city until further notice."

"I really have no plans to do so," I said. "You can call Mr. George if you'd like me to answer any more questions. I'm sure we can arrange a meeting if need be."

The chief inspector was not happy, but there was nothing he could do. He would simply have to pursue the proper channels. I'm sure our friend Mr. George would do a great job of putting up a wall to keep our visitors out.

There was something curious about Mr. George. When he was helping me up the stairs. I noticed a signet ring on his left hand. It was a gold ring with a black signet and some emblem on it. I noticed him fidgeting with the ring when we were talking in the study. It appears Mr. George has a personal interest in this case. He seems to be obsessed with this house and that door even more than poor Agatha. But the young Mr. George seems to have some kind of fixation with wanting to know what's on the other side of that door.

Mr. George said his goodbyes. The chief inspector went back to work on the body. And I walked back to the house and stood just inside the patio doors to watch them. They eventually loaded the body onto a gurney and wheeled it out to the coroner's vehicle. The entire process took a few hours.

It was getting late in the afternoon by the time they finished. Most of the police officers had left by 4 or 5 o'clock. Only two remained standing guard outside the carriage house. I decided that this would be a good time to call Agatha. I hoped she would come to the house. I thought we should both talk here in the study.

I tried her at work, but there was no answer. I tried her cell phone, but it went straight to voicemail. I decided to leave her a text message and suggested that we meet at the house around 7pm. A few moments later I received a reply. 'I'll be there' it said.

∾

The kitchen was finished and in working order, so I decided to cook a meal for the two of us. I ran out, did some shopping, and when I arrived back home, I began preparing our meal. I thought salmon would be nice. I just hoped she liked fish.

The house was still cluttered with painting supplies, but the kitchen stove and sink were all clean and ready to use. I cleared the small kitchen table, and covered it with a clean drop cloth the painting crew had left behind. It would do as a good substitute for a tablecloth. I set the table and placed a candle in the middle. I opened a bottle of white wine and let it breathe for an hour or so. By the time the fish was done it was nearly 7pm. Some steamed asparagus as a garnish and voila. A very nice meal for two.

Just after 7pm. I heard a knock at the door. It was Agatha.

"Hello. Hello," I said. "Please do come in." I took her coat and bag.

"The house looks marvelous," she said. "I haven't seen it since winter."

We walked into the kitchen.

"Yes. It's taking shape. The interior will be finished in a week or two. As soon as the floors are sealed and waxed."

I sat Agatha at the table and began to serve our meal.

"Already? It's still summer."

"We are fastidious. We've all been hard at work. Would you like some wine?"

"Very much so."

I poured both of us some wine.

"I hope you like salmon," I said and I sat down to join her.

"This is delicious," she said. "Did you cook this yourself?"

"One of the benefits of being a bachelor is that you learn how to cook," I said.

"Well you've done well. This is very good."

"Honestly, the fish does most of the work. I go to a certain shop and they always have the very best."

Agatha paused for a moment.

"I noticed a police car outside. Is that for us?"

"I hoped we could enjoy our meal first," I said. "But yes."

"What's happened?"

"We've run into a little snag while working on the carriage house. A crew member unearthed what appears to be a body."

"A body?" Agatha's expression changed. She began to fidget again. "Whose?"

"I have no idea." I tried to make an excuse to calm her nerves. "It's apparently very old. I overheard one of the officers describe it as mummified remains."

"Do you think it was someone who lived here?"

"Well..." I said and I had to pause to think about it. "You did translate those journal passages describing some of the events that took place in this house. To be honest, I'm afraid there might be more than one body."

"You mean in the room behind the door." Agatha's eyed widened. A palpable fear took hold of her. "Andrew, please tell me you haven't opened it."

"No. Not yet," I said. "But the police might order us to break in. We have our lawyers doing everything they can to block them. But to be honest, it's only a matter of time before we get through that door. One way or another."

Agatha stopped eating. She got very quiet and put her hands onto her lap.

"Andrew?" she said. "Do you know what's on the other side of that door?"

"A room full of skeletons, I suppose." I tried to laugh it off, but Agatha became very serious.

"According to everything I've read in those journals, that door is some kind of portal to what they describe as another dimension in space and time."

"What?" I chortled out.

"Just listen," she said. "Those rituals were not only performed here in this house. They were also performed inside the pyramids of Egypt and in the Aztec and Myan pyramids in South America. At Stonehenge. On Easter Island. At Machu Picchu and several other ancient ruins around the globe.

"But right here, where this house was built, they say there was an ancient temple that predates nearly all of them. That there was evidence of ruins in France and Germany that were even older than the Sumerian Empire by at least a thousand years. Some as old as five or six thousand BC.

"And according to what was written in the journals we found upstairs in that closet, there is evidence that supports that this being that they are trying to resurrect might even be alien or from another world. They describe this being as 'the destroyer of worlds' with the ability to control space and time. And this spot, this very spot where this house was built, was a place on this earth very much like a gate that allowed this creature to travel from its world or dimension into our own."

"And what happens if we open the door?" I said.

"I'm not sure it is a door," she said. "I think it may be a portal that allows this creature to cross over into our plane of existence."

"Our plane of existence?" I burst out. "Agatha, this sounds unreal."

"I'm not sure what is on the other side of that door, but according to the person or persons who wrote those journals, that is how they described it. And the rituals that were performed in that room were supposed to open the portal. But something happened in the late 1930's that prevented them from being able to do it. According to the notes in the journal, that's when the door was sealed."

"What did the notes say?" I said. "Who did it? And why didn't they just open the door themselves?"

"I haven't had that part translated yet," she said. "It's written in the last journal. It appears those were the last events to be recorded before the door was sealed shut and the closet disappeared from record. But it happened sometime while Charles Duvall and Elizabeth Colt lived in the house. Have you had the wood in that door analyzed?"

"I did. Some months ago," I said. "They said the wood

came from some kind of Norwegian old growth forest. Maybe as early as 450 AD after the collapse of the Roman empire in Europe and the surrounding Isles."

"The door itself is part of the ritual," said Agatha. "The wood comes from an old Norse village that was sacked by the Bavarians. And it says in those journals that the actual wood used to make that door came from the Great Hall of a Norse tribe, with some references to Odin and Loki."

"The Norse gods?" I said.

"And that the door itself is imbued with magical powers. If they destroyed the door, they would destroy the portal. So, it's imperative that the door remains intact in order for the ritual to work."

"And here I am doing everything I can to protect it, as an architectural historian. And as an architectural historian, knowing that the wood is from ancient Norway and possibly linked to the Norse gods only makes me want to preserve its heritage even more."

"I think they chose you to open the door, Andrew," she said.

"Wait. Chose? Who Chose?"

"They knew that you would never allow them to destroy the door. They knew that your passion for historical preservation would prevent you from doing so… and I think they want you to be the one who opens it."

"Who wants me to open it, Agatha? Other than the fact that I'm an architectural historian, why would someone choose me, specifically, to open that door?"

"I don't know," she said.

"And who are these people you keep mentioning?" I said. "With the photographs and the images of the all-seeing eye? Who are they?"

"I only know what was written in those journals. The rituals and the incantations were all written in ancient

Sumerian and Babylonian. But most of the rest was written in either, German, English, or Dutch… and they describe some kind of secret society…"

"The Illuminati?" I broke in. "Come on, Agatha. I've heard the conspiracy theories well enough to know that the wealthy have had secret societies for centuries all so that they can maintain power and control over the rest of the world. I'm not an idiot, but I don't believe all of the rumors and it still doesn't answer why they would want me whoever they are."

"Have you heard of the Praetorians?" she said. "England was colonized by Rome and Rome helped to civilize Britain until the collapse of the Roman Empire in the mid to late fifth century AD. The Praetorians were like the gladiators who protected the Caesar and the Senate in Rome and all of the wealthy diplomats including the ones who were dispatched to colonize the British Isles. According to the journals, the people who performed the rituals in this house were all descendants of those ancient Praetorians trusted to guard their secrets."

"Praetorians? Roman gladiators?" I said.

"These people are dangerous, Andrew. They are some of the wealthiest families in all of England. I think they are using you to open the door."

"But, Agatha, why me? Any decent hack could get that door open without destroying it. It still makes no sense why they would choose me, of all people."

"So, you still haven't been able to get the door open, this whole time?"

"No. We've been stymied for months," I said. "On our last attempt, we had a locksmith, who also knew how to break into bank vaults and the like, come in and run a scope into the lock through the key hole."

"What did he find?" she said.

"That someone had filled the lock with molten lead and it's jammed the mechanism."

"You should burn it. Burn the whole house down if you have to, Andrew."

"Agatha, stop! You're not making any sense. I can't just burn it down. This is still company property. I'd go to prison for arson."

"That's still better than what's on the other side of that door."

"Listen, I've heard you ranting about this demon or whatever you want to call it giving you nightmares, but all it sounds like to me is that you need a good therapist."

"You've never seen images in your mind, Andrew?"

She stared at me intently. I paused.

"Andrew!!" she yelled.

"Some," I said. "I've had some visions, but not like your describing."

"What did you see, Andrew? Tell me."

"Look, what we've uncovered in those journals is horrible. You're the one that's been reading them and translating them and I think they are causing you serious emotional distress."

"Serious emotional distress?" she laughed. Then she got angry. She got up and lunged at me. We started to fight. "Whatever this thing is, Andrew, it doesn't just want to drive me mad. It wants to kill me. It wants to fucking eviscerate me! Tell me what you've seen! Andrew! Tell me!"

I finally managed to fight her off and hold her up against the door frame that leads to the foyer. I could see the door to the cellar behind her. She turned her head to look at it and smiled at me.

"You know," she said. "Don't you"

"I don't know," I said letting her go. "I don't know if

what is in my head is real or not. It just seems like a dream to me. But it's not trying to hurt me, Agatha."

We sat down on the floor. Both of us out of breath. Agatha took my hand and pulled me close.

"Just tell me. So that I know I'm not insane."

"Alright," I said. "I see…I see people… in this house… having dinner parties. I see the people being mutilated at those rituals. I see people in purple robes standing in a circle chanting something demonic."

"The Praetorians," said Agatha.

"I don't know who they are," I said.

"And the door? What about the door? What's inside the door, Andrew?"

"I'm not sure. I've felt something, since the first day I was here. Like a black and swirling mist… but it's not real. These are just images in my imagination and tricks of the mind."

Agatha came closer and held my head to her chest.

"That's what I thought at first, too," she said "That my mind was playing tricks on me. But I'm not so sure anymore. I think it's more real than either of us fully realize."

Agatha's touch was so soft. So gentle. I couldn't stop myself from holding her. I drew her in close and nuzzled her neck. She stroked my hair and kissed my head. Before I knew it, we were kissing each other. We went upstairs to the bedroom and lay on the bed. We kissed as we undressed each other. Agatha got on top of me. In my mind I could hear swing music. A woman's voice sang:

"I need your love so badly. I love you oh so madly. But I don't stand a ghost of a chance with you. I thought at last I'd found you. But other love surrounds you. And I don't stand ghost of a chance with you."

I looked at Agatha and she was surrounded by pink and purple ethereal light. I enveloped her in my embrace and we began to make love. It was frenzied. It was ecstatic. As we grew more passionate, the music grew louder and the tempo grew faster, matching our rhythm. Pounding. Pounding. Pounding. Something was pounding on the door. We climaxed. And the pounding stopped. The music stopped. The lights grew dim. And we fell asleep.

∼

I awoke the next morning and Agatha was gone. She left a note. 'Burn it down,' it said. I went into the bathroom and took a shower. A very long hot shower and went downstairs for breakfast.

A week later Mr. George called. He wanted me to stop by the office and give a deposition. I hopped the train and went to the office.

"Thank you for coming in," Mr. George said. I took a seat in front of his desk. There was another man sitting next to the wall. "This is my colleague, Champion Douglas."

"Champion?" I said. "How do you do?"

"I've lived with it my whole life," he said. "Just call me Mr. Douglas."

"Mr. Douglas then," I said.

"Well, I'll get straight to it," Mr. George said. "The police would like to inspect the house and the rest of the yard. But they haven't sufficient evidence to gather a warrant... yet. Once they hear about the door, that might give them enough probable cause to go to a judge. In which case we've already prepared an injunction that would declare the door an historic artifact requiring specialized care in its opening and its removal if necessary... which of course, our firm, would conduct. We're going to block any third parties from gaining access to the house or the door."

"How soon do you think you can get it open?" Mr. Douglas asked. He was seated in an armchair with both of his hands resting on a cane held between his legs. I noticed that on his left hand he wore a gold and black signet ring very similar to Mr. George's ring.

"Well, that depends," I said. "Surely it's only a matter of time. Our most recent experts were able to determine how and why the lock was jammed."

"And?" said Mr. Douglas.

"Apparently, molten lead was poured through the keyhole and into the lock mechanism binding all of it together and rendering it inoperable."

"What about the rest of the house?" he said. "Is it almost finished?"

"Yes, about that," I said. "We are only weeks away from finishing the home. If we could get back to work right away, as soon as possible, that would help out greatly."

"We spoke with the medical examiner," said Mr. George. "The body is estimated to be nearly 100 years old. An elderly female apparently in her late 60's to early 70's."

"They can be that accurate in their determination?" I said.

"Yes. The forensic science is quite good," said Mr. George. "The point is there is no connection to any currently open case. That body could be anybody. Which means that there is no immediate reason to search the house."

"But we're going to allow it," said Mr. Douglas.

"Allow it?" I said. "But why?"

"Because we're going to make a deal with the police," he said. "We cannot hide the fact that the door is there and that it is, for the moment, impenetrable. We will allow them to inspect the rest of the house and the surrounding yard, so that you can get back to work finishing the restoration.

"We'll file the injunction protecting the door to give you more time to find a way to get it open. If you do so, in a timely manner, this will all go away very easily. So long as they find nothing damning in the room behind the door. Even if they find another mummified body in there, it might give the police something to do with their time, but it won't hinder us in finishing the house and selling it."

"I've got a lead on a company who uses high tech lasers, water drills, and the like that may be able to chip away at that lock," said Mr. George.

"Well... we want to preserve the lock mechanism as much as possible," I said.

"We'll see what we can do," said Mr. Douglas.

"And," said Mr. George. "We've hired our own company to work with the police using ground penetrating radar in the yard and the areas surrounding the house to look for any more bodies buried out there. And the same company has some very sophisticated sonar equipment that they can use to create a 3D image of the contents of the room behind the door.

"If there are more remains in the room. We will be able to notify the police and still be able to protect the door with the injunction. We have sworn testimony from over a dozen former occupants of the house who can attest that the door has remained sealed for almost 100 years. So, the police will have no reason to open the door except to collect the remains and identify the bodies. If there are any."

"Well, that sounds marvelous," I said. "How soon do you think we can get back to work."

"According to the medical examiner, there is no reason for them to go back to the site," said Mr. George. "They're going to let the inspectors have one more crack at it before allowing us access.

"It will be a day or two for the company I hired to

coordinate with the police and they will be able to inspect the yard and surrounding property in a few days. A separate crew with the sonar equipment will create a 3D map of the room behind the door at the same time and that should only take a few hours. If they don't find anything, it'll be, maybe a week or two before work can continue on the house. So, hopefully less than three weeks."

"Can work continue inside the house?" I said. "While they search the yard?"

"That would be up to the chief inspector," said Mr. Douglas. "I'll see what I can do."

Mr. Douglas got up, shook my hand, and left.

"Well, this should all go away within a month's time," said Mr. George.

"That sounds just wonderful," I said.

"I spoke with Theresa at UCL," he said.

"Oh, did you?" I said. The tenacious Mr. George. "What did she say?"

"Well, after she shared her enthusiasm for the rarities in the find, she said that that house was filled with horrors and that it should be condemned."

"Did she now?" I said.

"I don't share in her opinion though. I think it's a fine house. With a long history."

"Well," I said. "What should I include in the deposition?"

Mr. George very carefully guided me as to what information to include in my deposition and which topics to avoid. I simply followed his instruction and did as I was told.

The police came by to inspect the house and the surrounding property. After a day or two the company Mr. George hired began scanning the yard, accompanied by the police. To my knowledge nothing was found except for some old gardening tools buried next to the fence.

The company was also able to create a 3D image of the room behind the door. And it appeared to be nearly empty; with only some old chairs and other furniture inside, and a few lumps of cloth on the floor. Nothing to suggest a body, but they said they would have to come back with more sensitive equipment if we wanted to know what was in those lumps of cloth on the floor. I left it to the lawyers and the police to determine what to do next.

∼

Mr. George contacted the company he mentioned who might be able to get through that lock without damaging it or the door. A few days later the locksmith with the high-tech lasers stopped by the house. He was an odd man. In his thirties… wearing coveralls and a very complicated looking set of glasses on his head. He left his work van parked in the street and came in carrying a large black case in each arm. He didn't say a word. He just said hello and presented his card.

I led him into the cellar and to the door. He dropped his bags and immediately lowered the glasses onto his face. They seemed to be microscopes of some sort. He studied the lock intensely for a few moments before opening one of the cases. He took out a long black flexible tube, turned something on, and placed the tube within the lock.

"Yeah, I see it," he said. "Hardened lead gumming up the works. Not the best work at sabotage. An amateur more than likely. We might try very high vibrations. To knock some of it loose. And whatever we can't get that way we'll chip at with a laser. How important is it not to damage the lock?"

"Very… important," I said. "We want to preserve the mechanism if possible."

"Do you want it to remain functional?" he said, not removing his eyes from the camera or the door.

"That would be ideal," I said. "If at all possible."

"That's not always possible. We usually reach a point where we have to remove a gear, a pin, or a spring in order to get the lock to move."

"I see," I said. "Well, at first try, try to keep the entire mechanism intact and we'll see if it is still in working order."

"And if not?"

"I guess we'll just have to wait and see and go from there."

He raised his glasses and looked at me.

"What is it with you and this door? Why not just smash it with a hammer?"

"Well… I'm an architectural historian," I said. "And the wood in this door dates back to 450 AD and the Norse. With possible ties to Odin and Loki. The lock itself is as old as the house."

"The Norse gods?" He lowered his glasses again and inspected the door. "Well that is special isn't it? I'll have to be careful."

And with that he returned to his work without saying another word. He came and went for days. Bringing with him various devices and tools and he simply whittled away at the lead that was jamming the lock.

∽

As far as the home was concerned, the structural work was complete within a month's time. The carriage house was finished. The walls and floors were finished. All that was left now were the furnishings and decorations. I submitted my bid for the home with the firm. Chad was ecstatic. In a few weeks I would sign the lien and begin to use the home as my own personal residence.

It was mid-September. I walked around the home in its finished condition, room by room. It was quite remarkable. A very beautiful home. All of the wall treatments and wainscoting were finished. The floors were sealed and waxed. Several of the rooms were already furnished. The cost of the home, now completed, would place it at £1,500,000.

I stopped by the office at least twice a week. Chad said that the partners were very happy that the home was finished and that some of them would like to see it before it was sold. I told them to drop by anytime and the secretary put them into the schedule. One by one, over the course of a week or so, the partners stopped by, usually in the afternoon after lunch, and toured the house. Some of them went on about the door in the cellar. They seemed to have a particular interest in the door and its history. I didn't know what to tell them, so I just kept my mouth shut about the closet, the journals, or the door.

As luck would have it, Amanda arrived back in England that week. We made plans for her to come visit the house. She came over one morning to see the home. I hired a chef to serve us lunch. Eggs and crepes. After lunch, we again toured the house.

The master bathroom, guest bathroom, small guest room, and linen closet were all finished. The master bedroom and large guest bedrooms were still a work in progress.. The sun room, the dining room, and the parlor were nearly complete. And the study, the library, and the billiard room were all finished. As was the kitchen.

Slowly, the house was becoming a home. I did manage to preserve and reuse the gas lighting as I had intended, for the hallway sconces, staircase, foyer, and front entry.

Rebecca was able to find the perfect club chairs and

smoking table for the study in front of the fireplace. I had my own desk. All in all everything was moving along quite well. I had even begun moving my books into the library.

Amanda and I enjoyed our little tour of the house. We walked through the yard to the now finished carriage house.

"Are you going to park a horse and buggy out here?" she said. "To complete the look."

I laughed.

"I thought about it, but no," I said. "I think I'll park my car and bicycle in it."

"Why not a motorcycle?"

"Perhaps. If I can find one old enough."

"Old? Why an old one?"

"I just love old things, I suppose."

We walked back into the house through the patio and I poured each of us a glass of wine. But before I could hand her a glass, Amanda stopped me.

"Can I see the cellar?" she said. "You said it was too dark last time."

"Well, yes. I suppose. It's just a cellar. Utilities and all."

"Just the same." And then she paused. "You mentioned a door."

I didn't remember mentioning a door.

"Yes. There is a very old door in the cellar," I said. "We still haven't been able to get it open."

"This whole time?" she said. "Even though the rest of the house is finished?"

"Yes. Oddly enough, it's jammed. The lock is broken. But the door itself is quite old. An historic artifact, in fact. So, we've been taking our time as not to damage it or the lock."

She went down the stairs and straight to the door. She rubbed it with both hands.

"What do you think it's made of," she said.

"An ancient Norwegian timber," I said. "We had it analyzed. It dates back to the Norse with possible ties to Norse mythology."

"Like Odin and Thor?"

She seemed genuinely excited.

"Well, Odin and Loki, it seems. There was no mention of Thor in what I was told."

"Loki? The god of mischief and magic?" she said and laughed.

"We're not sure how true the rumors are," I said. "It was just mentioned by a colleague."

"By who?"

She was now admiring the lock and the iron pull ring.

"A research assistant."

"And you trust this person?"

"Well I do, but not on this particular subject, no. The ties to the Norse gods might just be rumor or conjecture. But the actual construction of the door itself is quite authentic. It's been checked by two sets of experts."

"And how old is it?"

She leaned back holding the iron pull ring.

"The timbers date from the mid fifth century AD. The iron bands and the lock date back to the late 18th century."

"Marvelous."

She gave the door one last stroke with her hand

"Make love to me," she said.

"What?" I said.

"Right now. I don't want anyone to know." She looked up the stairs to the foyer. She leaned me up against the door and kissed me. "Down here."

"In the cellar?"

"Why not? It's private."

She got undressed and pulled me towards her. Amanda

was relentless. She thrust her tongue down my throat and scratched my back. She tore my shirt off and licked my chest. She seemed possessed. She lowered me to the floor right in front of the door, tore open my pants, and climbed on top of me. Then she mounted me and began to writhe rhythmically.

Flashes of noise and light filled my mind. Visions of a train screeching to a halt. It was a tube stop. Amanda clawed at my chest and began to thrust herself onto my organ over and over again.

More lights flashed. In my mind, I saw Agatha step near the edge of the platform waiting for a train. Then I saw a group of people in purple and white robes all chanting rhythmically. The images began to spin in my mind.

Amanda grew louder and wilder as she pounded herself against me. The chanting grew louder. 'Eso To Gat Ether Hume.' The door began to pulse and breathe. A man in a black leather coat walked up behind Agatha. A gold and black signet ring on his left hand. 'Eso To Gat Ether Hume,' the people in robes chanted over and over again. Louder and louder. The man stood right behind Agatha and pushed. I climaxed. And Agatha's body fell in front of a train. I was in a delirium. Amanda sighed, produced a knife and cut her left palm. She rubbed her bloody hand on the door.

"Eso To Gat Ether Hume," she cried.

She moaned and rubbed herself against my body. I passed out. When I woke, I was dressed and sitting at the kitchen table. Amanda had just returned from the bathroom upstairs, cleaned and dressed. A white bandage on her right hand. She kissed me on the head.

"I'll call you," she said as she grabbed her things and left.

I didn't know what happened. How on Earth did I get

back upstairs? I remembered the visions of Agatha. The phone rang.

"Yes, hello," I said.

It was Shelly from the office.

"Hello, Andrew." She sounded like she had been crying. "Am I disturbing you?"

"No. No. It's quite alright. Did something happen? You sound upset."

"It's Agatha," she said. "She fell in front of a train. They think it's suicide."

"Suicide?" I said.

"They found a note in her pocket."

"Poor Agatha."

"You worked with her, Andrew. The police want to ask you a few questions."

"The Police?" I said. "Phone Mr. George our lawyer."

"Who?" said Shelly

"A Mr. Stephen George."

"We don't have a Mr. George on staff."

"What about a Mr. Douglas? Champion Douglas?"

"We don't have a Mr. George or a Mr. Douglas on our team of lawyers at the firm," said Shelly.

"But I don't understand. I spoke with them at the office."

"There is no one with those names on our legal team." Then she paused for a moment. "Can I call someone for you? A doctor perhaps," she said.

∼

I just hung up the phone and sat down. Agatha was dead. What happened? I remembered the images I saw in my mind. The man in the black leather jacket wearing the gold signet ring. The police phoned an hour later and said that they would be at the home around 5pm. They wanted to question me on the premises.

I had no lawyer. I didn't know what to say. Who was Mr. George? Or Mr. Douglas for that matter? How could they not work for the firm? We met in an office at the firm, in front of everybody. I must admit, I have never worked closely with the legal department. I had spoken with their lawyers from time to time, but I did not know any of them intimately. If they were imposters how were they let into the building? Who did they really work for?

I went back into my briefcase to get out Agatha's notes, but the manila envelope was gone. I double checked to see if it was in my bag. But it wasn't. I looked in the desk. Nothing. I stared out the window of my study. The police would be here around 5pm. I had nearly 3 hours before they arrived.

There was a knock at the door. It was the strange locksmith with the glasses, here again with yet another black case.

"Hello," I said, as I let him in.

He nodded and went straight to the cellar without saying a word. He didn't even acknowledge that he was coming into my house. He simply walked right past me. I followed him to the stairs and into the cellar.

"I needed a heating torch," he said. "There's quite a bit of debris. In the lock, that is." He lowered his glasses and took out yet another piece of machinery.

"How long do you think this will take you?" I said. He stopped by a few days each week. Always with a new piece of equipment. With still no word on his progress. Other than…

"It's going," he said. "The machinery is delicate to say the least. And old. It's a complicated tumbler. But without being able to see the moving parts, I have no idea how to disengage the lock. You can only see so much with a scope and a magnifying glass."

"So what are you able to do?" I said.

"I'm slowly clearing the lead from the mechanism. Piece by piece. An inch at a time. There's a lot of it. the entire lower half of the lock chamber is filled with hardened lead. It's in between all of the pieces of the lock. If I try too hard or go too fast it will break or disable the lock. And you had mentioned the importance of keeping the lock intact. So I'm making the best progress that I can."

He said nearly the same thing every time. At first it made sense. But after hearing it three or four times it sounded a bit rehearsed. And he never said anything else other than hello or goodbye. He'd come in a few days each week never more. He'd work for a few hours each time and then leave. Every time he'd say he needed a different piece of equipment. And each time he'd return with a different piece of equipment.

I had the habit of watching him work from time to time. He's tried machinery, chemistry, cold, heat. He's being very methodical and thorough. He hasn't seemed to break the lock yet or to get it open. So I've simply been patient with him.

Just as always, the man came in, worked for a few hours, and left without saying a word. This time, as he passed me in the foyer on his way out, he reached up and scratched the back of his neck. I noticed a small tattoo to the left side of his neck, just above the nape. A triangle, with some kind of object in the center. But I barely saw it and couldn't tell what it was. It was just past 5 o'clock when he left, and as he passed me in the foyer to leave, the police walked in the front door. Odd timing, I thought.

∽

"Hello," the chief inspector said.

He showed me his badge. Then he opened and rebuttoned his jacket. I got a glimpse of the pistol he carried at his waist. His partner showed me his credentials as well.

"Shall we meet in the study?" I said and motioned for them to follow me. The chief inspector went into the study and had a seat in front of my desk. His partner walked to the back of the room near the fireplace and began to inspect some of the books on the shelf. I sat at the desk and tried to keep an eye on them both, but in the next moment the other inspector entered the billiard room and vanished out of sight.

"We've been having a difficult time, Mr. Martin," the chief inspector said.

"A difficult time?" I said. "With what?"

"You're stalling us by not allowing us to get into that room in the cellar. And now we have two murders associated with this house since you were the person who took possession of it."

"I am the person overseeing the historic restoration of the entire house and its grounds to restore it to period and to preserve its architecture and history as a qualified professional at the head of my field. It has been my career for over two decades and this house is no exception whether I make use of it as my own personal home or not.

"In either case it is my duty and responsibility to my colleagues and to my firm to do the very best at my job and if you look at the home in its present condition, I have done just that. And I am sorry that a mummified body over 100 years old was found on the grounds. It may have easily been a family burial and not a murder. But that has nothing to do with me or my firm to the best of my knowledge.

"I did not murder anyone. And I am sorry to say that poor Agatha may very well have been suicidal and her death may have simply been a tragic accident on her part."

"Suicidal?" said the chief inspector. "No one said she was suicidal. Who have you been talking to?"

"Shelly. The secretary at the office," I said. "She called me earlier and informed me of Agatha's untimely demise. She mentioned a suicide note that was found in her pocket."

"We don't think it was suicide," he said. "We have no way to authenticate the note."

"I see," I said. "So I'm a suspect?"

"Where were you at 11:00am this morning?" he said.

I thought to tell him about Amanda and realized I never knew her last name. I asked one time, but she didn't seem to hear me, then she talked about her family and I forgot to ask again. This morning she said that she didn't want anyone to know that she was here.

I suddenly remembered when she was writhing on top of me like a snake. At one point she lowered herself to me and I held her close, looking over her shoulder. And on the back of her shoulder I saw what appeared to be a triangle, only I saw it upside down. It was the same symbol that was on the strange locksmith's neck.

"Mr. Martin," the chief inspector said.

I snapped out of it.

"Yes?"

"Where were you at 11:00am this morning?" he repeated.

"I was here, actually," I said. "Having lunch with a guest."

"And who was your guest?"

"A woman I recently started dating. I barely know her. Her name is Amanda."

"And does Amanda have a last name?" He wrote notes

into his notepad as we talked. I looked across the foyer and saw the other inspector in the parlor. He was slowly making his way through the house.

"If she does, I don't know it. I never asked."

"And how do you know this woman?" He flipped the page in his notebook and held his pen ready to record more notes.

"That's private," I said. "You'd have to ask her yourself."

"Excuse me?" he said. "Are you being uncooperative in a murder investigation? Do you want me to place you under arrest so that we can finish this conversation in the interrogation room?"

"No. That will not be necessary," I said. "I'm sorry if I were being cheeky. But you will simply have to find her and ask her yourself. I know nearly nothing about the woman. We've only met a few times. A colleague at work introduced us. That's all I know."

He sat there and nodded.

"So you were having lunch with this woman, Amanda at 11:00am this morning? Are there any witnesses to support your story?"

"Actually, yes. The cook. She is the one who prepared the meal for us."

"And what was her name?"

"I don't know," I said. "Sally or something. I phoned a caterer I've worked with before and requested a personal chief. They sent whoever was available this morning. She left right after we finished eating at about noon."

"And do you have the number for this caterer?"

"Of course." As I reached for my rolodex, I looked into the foyer and noticed the other inspector ascending the stairs into the upper floors. I went through the rolodex on my desk, found the number for the caterer, and handed it to the chief inspector.

"You actually use one of those?" He pointed at the rolodex with his pen.

"It helps me stay organized," I said. "What can I tell you? It works."

"But everyone uses computers nowadays. Email? Cell phones?"

He made a gesture with his hand as if he we talking into an invisible phone.

"I'm old fashioned," I said. "If you lose electricity you lose your contacts. I'd simply rather use real paper."

"Old fashioned?" he said. "Architectural historian?" He pointed at me with his pen. "Performing an historic restoration on a house? With a mysterious door in the cellar, that no one has been able to get open for more than a year?"

"Yes," I said. "That is correct."

"Anything happen in this house within the past year that was out of the ordinary?"

"Well you see, this is getting within the confidentiality of the firm and I am not allowed, for legal reasons, to allow others not pertinent to its discovery to have any information on it."

"On a discovery?" he said. "Made in this house?"

"Yes," I said.

"That you've kept a secret?"

"No. It's been held within strict confidence. Very much like the door in the cellar."

"The door in the cellar? The one you won't allow us to open?"

"Well, no. Our firm is doing our best to open the door without damaging it or the lock," I said. "That door has been found to have exceptionally rare and valuable meaning. It should by all rights be removed and placed in a museum of architectural history along with the pharaohs' tombs and the holy cross. It really is that valuable in its intracity and uniqueness. It is in the process of being declared an historic artifact that must be preserved.

"So yes, a discovery of valuable import. And we've simply found that the history of the house is not only unique, it is vital and necessary for us to document because of what we've found within it. But it's confidential, and we tell no one not absolutely pertinent about the discovery until we've had adequate time to document our own findings.

"It's like discovering gold in the Rockies. Or uncovering a Renaissance masterpiece buried deep within someone's barn that no one knew about. So, I am sorry, but it is professional etiquette that absolutely no one know about it until we catalogue our findings. I assure you that it is all perfectly legal and we have no need to hinder you in your progress in answering your own questions and finding your own answers. But I don't know them.

"I'm an architectural historian. We've just recently acquired the house and I was the one chosen to conduct the restoration. So, I am above all proud of our discovery. But it's not my news to share. There are entire firms and agencies and universities who want to keep this private. And they all have their own lawyers who will ensure that these matters do stay private. And that is not me trying to stop you from doing your job. This is my job. And I have legal grounds to do so. It's all company property. The discovery. Not mine. I just live here. I don't even own the home yet."

"So, this is not your personal residence?"

He put down his pen and notepad.

"No. Not yet. I plan to purchase the home, but it is still company property. The paperwork hasn't even been finalized yet. I am simply the person whose job it was to restore the house to period accuracy. I am a highly qualified professional I might add."

"I'm sorry," he said. "I didn't mean to insult you or your firm, but this is a murder investigation. A body was found on the premises. And a young woman died earlier today. A woman you know. A woman who mentioned one Mr. Andrew Martin in a note that was found in her pocket."

He produced a note from his jacket pocket, sealed in plastic, and placed it on the desk. I went to read it, but he picked it up and put it back into his pocket.

"That is you, isn't it? Mr. Martin?"

"I have no idea what is written in that note," I said. "I only knew that she was delirious or something. I thought she needed a therapist. And I was afraid for her."

"Is there any reason, that you know of, why she would be this way?"

"She was the person who made the discovery in the house."

I felt a bit of shame when I said it.

"Why would this upset her?" said the chief inspector. "Shouldn't she be proud of her discovery? You said that you and your firm were proud of this discovery. If she was the one who discovered it, why wasn't she the most excited about it?"

"Because she thought she was being haunted by something," I said and immediately wished I hadn't.

"Haunted?" he said. "By a ghost? In this house?"

"Well, yes. But it wasn't a ghost that Agatha described… It was a demon."

"A demon?" He picked up his pen and notepad again.

"I am not sure that I am qualified to talk about this. I am not a licensed therapist. I have no idea in what state of mind she was in when she first told me about it, just months after the discovery. Or why she said what she did the last time that I saw her."

"What did she say, the last time you saw her?" He readied his pen.

"She left a note," I said. "It said, 'burn it down,' and nothing else."

"Burn it down? Burn what down?"

The chief inspector was getting agitated.

"The house," I said. "She said that she was being haunted by a demon that we uncovered within the house. She said that it was being held back by the door in the cellar. And she said that it was not only trying to drive her mad, but that it was also trying to kill her. In her exact words she said that it felt like this thing wanted to 'eviscerate' her. In what state of mind do you have to be in to say that to someone and believe it?"

The inspector stopped writing.

"Can I see the door?" he said.

He put away his notepad and pen. A policeman in uniform came in from the front door and told the chief inspector something in his ear.

"Are the police here as well?" I said. "I thought this was a casual conversation."

"It's just a precaution," said the chief inspector. "Agatha's body just left autopsy."

My stomach turned. Agatha was dead. She really was dead and I am one of the last people who saw her alive. As the other policeman turned to leave, I noticed a triangle on his right wrist above the cuff.

"So can we see the door now please?" said the chief inspector.

"Yes. Of course," I said. "This way."

I entered the foyer and the other inspector was already at the head of the stairs to the cellar. I looked out the front door and there was a squad car outside with two policemen on the porch. 'That's a lot of security,' I thought. I went in first, hit the light switch and descended the stairs. It was cool and damp in the cellar. It was well into autumn and the weather had begun to change. I stood in front of the furnace to allow both gentlemen to get near the door.

"This is the door?" the chief inspector said.

"Yes, but please don't touch it," I said as politely as possible. "Remember it's an historic artifact."

The other inspector said something into the chief inspector's ear.

"Whose blood is this?" the chief inspector said pointing at the spot on the door where Amanda rubbed her bloody hand.

"Blood?" I said. "I meant the door. I don't know whose blood that is, but we will have to have a team of experts remove the blood from the door as carefully as possible without disturbing the surface of the door. As I said it is an historic artifact absolutely no one who is not professionally qualified may touch the door."

"But there's blood on it," the chief inspector said.

"But it could be from anyone who has been working on the house this entire time," I said.

The other inspector said something else into the chief inspector's ear.

"It looks pretty recent," the chief inspector said. Then he asked his partner. "How recent?"

"Very recent," the other inspector said.

I remembered the bandage on Amanda's right hand.

"Do you know whose blood this is on the door, Mr. Martin?" the chief inspector said.

"I think I do," I said "Amanda did that, earlier today, after lunch." I said pointing at the door.

"The mysterious Amanda, that nobody knows about?"

"Except for Shelly at the office," I said. "Although I'm not sure how they know each other."

"You don't know how your office colleague Shelly and

this mysterious woman Amanda know each other?" he said waving his hand in the air. "And why not?"

"I never know who these women Shelly introduces me to are?" I said.

"Excuse me? Did you say that your office colleague was in the habit of finding you women? Women who rub blood on thousand year old doors?"

"Wait? What? No," I said shaking my head. "She fixed me up on dates from now and again."

"With women that you did not know?" he said. "And where did she find these women that you did not know?"

"I honestly don't know where she found them," I said. "I stopped asking. Sometimes she meets perfect strangers and tries to give them my number."

"And who is Shelly at the office," he said.

"The secretary," I said. "She works at the firm."

"Is she your secretary?"

"No. No. She's the company secretary. She works at the office. I only know her from work."

"And this secretary, Shelly, sets you up on dates from time and again, with women she doesn't even know herself and has just recently met?"

"Yes," I said. "She thinks she's helping me. And although I avoid it as much as possible, sometimes I go on dates with these women. It doesn't always work out."

"Are you lonely? Mr. Martin?" he said. "Are these call girls?"

"What? No," I said. "I hope not. I never asked. I just assumed they were friends of hers."

"And were they attractive?"

"Some were very attractive," I said. "Come to think of it, Shelly has very good taste in women. They were all very nice and many were attractive."

"And how many dates did you go on?" the chief inspector said.

"Not many," I said. I was beginning to get angry. "I'm a bachelor. I'm allowed to have a good friend who fixes me up on dates from time and again so that I don't die of loneliness. I'm middle aged and unmarried. She cares for me and doesn't want me to die an old man with nothing but a beautiful house. These matters are private."

"Are these questions too personal for you, Mr. Martin?" the chief inspector said.

"Yes. They are intrusive," I said.

The chief inspector lost his patience.

"Were you intimate with the late Agatha Cooper before she died this morning? Was your privacy worth her life because you and your firm wanted to keep this discovery of hers a secret?"

I was stymied. I painted myself into a corner and drew a target on my chest. I'm not a lawyer. I made myself a suspect.

"No," I said. "Absolutely not. But I do not know what state of mind she was in at the time of her death."

"Were you, at any time, intimate with Agatha Cooper during the entire time that she was employed by you or your firm?"

"These matters are private," I said. "I'll need to consult my attorney."

"You may have an attorney present at your questioning," he said. "We'll get a warrant to inspect the house."

"At my questioning? Honestly, I employed her. We were friends. We got along. We did what friends do. And now she's gone and I've got you two bleeding assholes trying to say that I am somehow responsible for her death. I knew her enough to know that I loved her as a person and as a friend and that this is a tragic loss for all of us who actually knew her, and you two are acting like a couple of pricks. Have some feeling for the people who actually knew and cared for her, you insensitive pricks. Get out of my house."

"We still have a few more questions," he continued.

"And you have enough answers," I said. "Come back with a warrant."

"We're going to need you to come with us to the station for questioning," he said.

"And I would like to phone my attorney," I said.

∼

The chief inspector handcuffed me and placed me in the back of the squad car. They took me to the police station, but I wasn't charged with anything. I was merely detained for questioning as a possible suspect. I didn't know who to call, so I called my friend Jack who was a lawyer and a personal friend. His father was my father's lawyer and we all got along. He wasn't a criminal lawyer, but he'd know who to call.

The police put me in a holding cell and kept me handcuffed the entire time. I couldn't even take a shit if I had to because of these bastards. I was there a couple of hours before Jack arrived with a colleague he knew. I was detained and questioned. My attorney advised me on what to say, and in the end, the police had no direct evidence linking me to any crime so they had to let me go.

I don't know why, but when I was released I simply went back to the house. The police were there. I stayed outside on the pavement and stared at it. Was it a home? Would it be my home? With the history that it has, could I ever make it a home?

Jack told me not to go into the house until the police had inspected it. He said to let the police find everything themselves and let them prove their case; to let them collect their forensic evidence and stay out of their way. He also said to be as cooperative as possible and just plead innocence. Which all sounded great, until I remembered the images of that man in the black coat pushing Agatha in front of the train.

Was that knowledge criminal? Was it a dream? An hallucination? I saw it as clear as day. I could remember every detail. The tube stop. Her standing at the edge. With her head down. She looked unkempt. Her hands were shaking. The man in the black leather jacket came up behind her. As the train pulled into the station, he stepped in and pushed her over the edge. I could see his hands when he did it. He wore a black signet ring.

Was I remembering this or was I having hallucinations? What kind of visions were these? Was I on some kind of drug? Did I pass out? How did I get back upstairs?

I decided to take the train back to my apartment. The manila envelope Agatha had given me was gone. All of the information and evidence I had about who these people were was gone.

The police said that she mentioned me in a note that was found in her pocket. Shelly said it was a suicide note, not the police inspector. Did she try to leave me anything else? I had no idea where her apartment would be. How else would she try to get in touch with me?

I had to see Theresa. What was written in that last journal? What else happened in that house? I called Theresa. She was still in her office. I told her to wait for me and took the train to UCL.

5

"Resurrect the Dead."

When I arrived, Theresa was in her office at her desk, as per usual.

"Is the professor in?" I said popping my head into the room.

Theresa got up and gave me a tearful hug.

"Oh, Andrew. The police called. They told me about Agatha. They're coming here tomorrow. They want me to come down to the station and answer some questions. And they told me to not to talk to you. But to hell with them. What happened?"

"I don't know." I sat down in a chair next to the door and tried to make sense of everything. "I believe that Agatha made some discoveries about the people responsible for whatever happened in that house and now some very dangerous people are after us because of our discovery there."

"Us? All of us? Because of the discovery? Everything

that we've been cataloguing?" Theresa wrung he fingers anxiously.

"I'm not sure, but I believe it has more to do with what was written in those journals about the people who lived in the house. The Praetorians, Agatha called them. She gave me an envelope with notes containing information on the families who lived in the house and translations of some of the rituals that were performed there."

"And where are the notes she gave you? maybe they can help."

"Gone. Taken. I looked for them earlier today, but they disappeared."

"Disappeared? You mean someone took them? But why?"

"To cover it up, I think." I paced the room trying to remember what was in Agatha's notes. "She made references to a secret society. She drew symbols of the all-seeing eye on photographs of the male owners of the home. She said that they were all related and that they all practiced the same occult religion."

"Demon worship?"

She tried not to sound too condescending.

"You didn't see her the way she looked when she came to see me. She wasn't the same. I thought she was having a nervous breakdown. But her notes were meticulous and she was deathly serious. She said that these were some of the wealthiest families in England."

I could see the look of disbelief on Theresa's face. I looked down at my shoes.

"Demons and secret societies? Andrew, you can't possibly expect me to believe any of that."

"I thought the same thing at first." I tried to put what I was thinking into words. I thought about the visions and hallucinations I had been experiencing ever since I first visited the house. "I know it sounds mad, but the house and these people might actually be who and what Agatha thought they were. And when she found out too much, they got rid of her."

"She was murdered? The police said that she fell in front of a train."

"I think she may have been pushed by a member of this secret society, the Praetorians. I think that there are more of them. I think some of them are in the police and that they have already been to the house."

"Some of them are policemen?" Theresa's patience ran out. "Andrew, this sounds like a lot of conspiracy theory nonsense. The all-seeing eye? The occult? The Praetorians? I have no idea what the two of you talked about, but Agatha did not tell me about any of this. I have no idea what was in those notes she gave you, but she never mentioned any of this to me."

"Theresa, please," I pleaded with her. "She worked with you for months after the closet was discovered. You saw her every day. She must have said something."

"Andrew, I read the journals, just as Agatha did. I do believe that whoever wrote them believed in what they were doing. But that was over a hundred years ago. You are asking me to believe that the same people still exist today. And that they murdered Agatha to cover all of this up. I'm sorry, but that's just too much to believe."

"But what if it's true, Theresa?" I tried to regain her confidence. "What if she was murdered? The only clue I have is what she has been researching in those journals."

"Her thesis?" she said.

"What?"

"After Agatha and I had finished cataloguing everything we found in the closet, we parted ways and conducted our research independently. I focused mainly on the artifacts and Theresa focused primarily on the journals. Eventually she approached the board to conduct her own research and applied for her thesis. It was approved over the summer. She's had her head buried in those journals ever since."

"I need to see them," I said. "The journals. Agatha told me, that the final clue to this puzzle was somewhere within the pages of the last journal that was written. I need to find out what that was."

"Did you do it?" Theresa asked coldly. "Did you kill her?"

"Of course not. How could you ask such a thing?"

"I had to see the look in your eyes when you answered. Don't worry I believe you."

"Well, I believe that I am being set up to take the fall for all of this, and that we all need to protect ourselves from whoever these people are. And it all has to do with those journals and that bloody door in the cellar."

I lost my patience and kicked the trash can.

"You're asking me to break the law, Andrew," Theresa said picking up the trash can and putting it back in its place. "I can see why the police told me not to talk to you. But I'm going to help you, because of what I saw happening to Agatha."

"Like what? What did you see?"

"Like signs of a nervous breakdown, as you described." Theresa stared at me for a few moments before she continued. "At first, when we were just cataloguing items, she seemed fine. Everything was normal. We even worked well together. She was both professional and meticulous just as you described. But after we were done cataloguing everything and she began to focus on studying and translating the journals, her demeanor changed. I thought it might have been work stress, but it got worse. The more she uncovered in those journals, the more paranoid she seemed to become."

"I think she had valid reasons to be paranoid," I finally

conceded. "I think that I am being manipulated by these people as well."

"What do you mean?"

"Agatha mentioned that these people, the Praetorians, had chosen me as the person to open the door in the cellar. That it was part of some ritual to resurrect an ancient Babylonian demon or god. And that this demon would cause the end of the world."

"Well, that's just ludicrous." Theresa sat back in her chair and stared at me.

"I thought the same thing, but then she died before she could tell my why and the only clue I have is what she was researching in those journals, specifically in the last one that was written." I stared at Theresa to meet her gaze. "I need your help."

"Well… I suppose we could have a look then. If it's that important to you."

Theresa grabbed her keys and we walked over to the warehouse where the artifacts were stored. On the way over, Theresa told me that the entire collection had its provenance approved and certified, and that she was now the official curator for the collection. Bittersweet news in light of recent events. I tried not to talk about it. We arrived at the warehouse and began to look around. Everything from the closet was laid out on tables and outlined with masking tape. Each item had a note card with its catalogue number and identification written on it.

"What are we looking for, Andrew?" Theresa asked placing her keys on the desk.

"The journals, I believe would be the best place to start. Where are they?"

"They should be on that table to the left," she said pointing to the far side of the room.

I walked over to the tables, to where the journals were located. There were five spaces for five journals, but only four were there. The fifth one, the last one, was missing.

"One's missing," I said. "I think it's the one we need."

"Those journals aren't allowed to leave the building, Andrew. It has to be here," she said crossing over to the table to help look. She ran her fingers over the empty space where the fifth journal should be. "That's odd. Nothing is allowed to be removed from these tables." She quickly searched the entire collection. The only thing missing was the journal.

"Is there anywhere else it could be?" I asked.

"Well, Agatha had a small office in the basement. She spent most of her time down there studying photocopies of pages from the journals. We could look there, I suppose."

Theresa grabbed her keys from the desk and we headed downstairs to the basement. On the way down, I thought about what Mr. George had said; that he had visited Theresa at UCL and when he asked her about the house, she said that it was a house full of horrors that should be condemned.

"Theresa, did a Mr. Stephen George come to visit you recently?" I asked.

"Who?"

"I'm not sure. He said he was a lawyer, but I'm afraid that might not have been true. He was curious about the discovery we made in the closet and I told him that if he wanted to know anything about it, that he would have to ask you directly."

"Andrew, we are not in the habit of giving out confidential information to strangers no matter who they are. We keep this facility under lock and key."

"I told him as much, which was odd, because he said that he did speak with you and that you said that the house was full of horrors and that it should be condemned."

"What?" Theresa seemed surprised, even frightened.

"I was curious to know, because I believe that he might be one of these people that Agatha described. A Praetorian. I was just curious if that was something you said or not."

"Stop it, Andrew." Theresa was visibly upset. "Are you purposefully trying to scare or intimidate me? What is all of this about?"

We stopped in the basement corridor and faced each other.

"He said he was a lawyer at my firm. This Mr. George. But no one at the firm has ever heard of him. He knows about the door. He knows about the closet. He seems to have some vested interest in getting that door in the cellar open. And he may very well be connected to everything that has been happening, including Agatha's death."

"Stop!" Theresa put her hand up. "Not a word more. I did say those things, Andrew. After I had read some of the translations from the journals. A particularly gruesome description about the decapitation and disembowelment of an infant."

"So, you saw him then? This Mr. George?" I asked.

"No. Not him. It was late. I was alone in my office. And there was something or someone in the hall outside my door. I have no idea what it was. I thought it might have been a dog. A very large black dog. I couldn't see it clearly. It was too dark. But I heard it, growling, or at least I thought it sounded like growling. But, I only noticed it was there after I said those things. As if it had heard me. When I finally gained enough courage to look outside into the hallway, it was gone. I have no idea who this Mr. George is, but that is not what I saw."

"Why didn't you mention it earlier?" I was a bit perturbed. "You accused both Agatha and I of being mad or obsessed with conspiracy theories when I tried to tell you about the Praetorians and this Babylonian demon, but you saw something. Agatha said that she saw something, too."

"I have no idea what it was, Andrew. I thought I had imagined it. Until you mentioned what this Mr. George heard me say." Then Theresa got defensive and stood face to face with me. "What about you, Andrew. What have you seen? What are you hiding?"

Just then we heard a noise. Like the sound of a glass bottle being kicked across the floor. We were both seized with fear.

"We should get to the office," she said.

"I wholeheartedly agree," I answered.

We made our way to Agatha's office as quickly as possible. Theresa unlocked the door, we entered and closed the door behind us as quickly and as quietly as possible, and locked it.

"What is going on, Andrew?" Theresa said as soon as the door was shut.

"I have no idea," I said. "Some kind of haunting, maybe?"

"A haunting?" Theresa folded her arms in front of her and paced the room. "The Praetorians? Babylonian demons? I don't understand."

"Agatha did," I said falling to my haunches on the floor. "I'm afraid she knew more than either of us could have possibly known about all of this. She even tried to warn me, but I didn't believe her. I didn't take her seriously, until after she died and they tried to pin her murder on me."

"Agatha's thesis?" Theresa said having a seat on the edge of the desk.

"It's all I've got," I said looking up at her. "Agatha said that the answers to all of this were written in that last journal."

"You still haven't told me Andrew. I saw that girl fall

apart over the months she spent reading those journals. What about you? How do I know you're not mad?"

"You don't," I said. "But what I've been experiencing is different from what she described. She said that this being, might be a creature from another dimension, and that it blamed her for waking it up. She said that it wanted to eviscerate her. And that it was being held back by the door in the cellar. She begged me to never open the door. To never let it out. She told me that I should burn the house down, to prevent this being from entering our world."

"A being from another dimension?" Theresa laughed out loud.

"I don't know if that's what it is. It's not the same creature that I've seen. Or that you've seen for that matter. I don't see an inter-dimensional demon or a big black dog. I see a woman. A beautiful woman."

"A woman? Ha! You are a pathetic and lonely man, Andrew. I'm sorry to say it aloud, but it's true. You always have been. You've barely dated anyone in the entire time I've known you. You're practically a recluse. So, when Agatha describes being haunted by a demon who wants to eviscerate her, and when I see some kind of evil black dog, you see a beautiful woman?"

"I don't know what I see." I stood up. "We're talking about things that may not even be real, Theresa. Are you saying that you really did see some kind of demon dog in your hallway? Am I to believe everything Agatha said about this thing or these people? I have just as many questions as you do. But I do believe that these people are real. The Praetorians. And I do believe that they may have murdered Agatha before she could find out the truth. And yes, I am a pathetic and lonely man, which is why no woman wanted to be with me all these years, I suppose."

"I'm sorry, Andrew," Theresa said. And she embraced

me. "I didn't mean to say those things. You must be terribly lonely."

"It's just my lot. I never tried to meet someone. I never tried to be in a relationship. I hoped that it would happen one day and it never did. That's all. But as far as I know, all of our lives could be in danger because of what we found in that house. And I'm afraid I'm being set up by these people, but I have no idea why."

"Agatha said that she thought you were chosen by these people? For what?"

"To open the door without destroying it. The door itself, as well as the lock, apparently, are all a part of this ritual. And if they destroy the door, they will destroy the portal that will allow this being to enter our world. So, it is imperative that the door and the lock remain intact for the ritual to work."

"And you're an architectural historian, whose duty it is to preserve such artifacts."

"Precisely. And it's true. I am doing everything I can to protect and to preserve that door."

"And Agatha said that she found the answers in the last journal?"

"I don't know. She said that it was the only one she hadn't translated yet. And that it was written during the time the door and the closet were both sealed shut. I assumed there would be an answer in there somewhere. But I haven't a clue what to look for."

"Well, I guess we had better find it then. If it's to be the fate of the world and all."

Theresa tried to laugh. So did I. We both started to look around the office. It was small. There were only two desks in it. Each had its own computer.

"Agatha used the desk on your side," said Theresa. "I'll check this one."

We both searched the office for any sign of the journal.

Agatha had left a notebook open on her desk. Her handwriting reminded me of a day we spent together at the house, before we discovered the closet. We were both standing at my makeshift desk in the study, going over the house plans while having some coffee. She wrote with these huge flamboyant loops and curves. Like something a teenager would write in her diary. Very feminine and playful.

I turned the page in her notebook and there was some sort of symbol drawn on it. Like a sun with rays of light shining down. Then I remembered the vision of her standing at the tube stop and the hands that pushed her over. The black signet ring on the left hand of the man who did it. And the symbol on that ring. A sun with rays of light shining down.

I turned to the next page. Agatha had drawn symbols of the all-seeing eye, as well as other sketches of eyes, only these eyes all had rays or beams of light below them, like the sun and its rays. I realized that they were the same thing. That these were all different renderings of the all-seeing eye.

I closed my eyes and tried to remember the triangle tattoos I saw on the strange locksmith's neck, on Amanda's back, and on the police officer's wrist. I thought it was a figure inside the triangle, but I realized that the triangle was actually a pyramid and that the image was the same rendering for the all-seeing eye. An eye with rays of light shining down. There wasn't anything else in or around the desk.

Theresa said that the other desk was empty. There was no closet in the room, but there were two lockers. She looked in the one on the left. It was empty. She looked in the one on the right and we saw Agatha's hoodie hanging inside, the one with the UCL logo on it. I walked over to the locker. Theresa began removing everything inside. Her hoodie, some books, and at the bottom, her backpack. We placed everything on the desks and started looking through them.

Theresa searched the hoodie and the books. I looked through the backpack. Her laptop was in it. A book on ancient Babylon. A notebook. And some pens. Nothing else. It was empty. I turned the backpack upside down to dump what was left inside onto the floor. But nothing fell out. No journal. I threw the backpack onto the desk.

"It's not here," I said.

"Are you sure?" said Theresa. "Look again."

I picked up the backpack again. I opened every pocket and looked inside. It was empty. I tossed the backpack back onto the desk.

"Where else could it be?" I said searching the room. But there was nothing else in the room except for some large photographs that hung on the walls. I took a closer look at each photograph. One was of Westminster Abby. Another of Paddington Station. And last of the Manchester Square Fire Station. Then I remembered her note.

"Burn it down," I whispered.

I looked at the picture of the fire station. I took it down and turned it over. I opened the back. Inside was an old photograph folded in half.

"What is it?" asked Theresa.

"A clue, I think."

I unfolded the photograph and looked at it. It was a picture of one of the families that lived at the house with a symbol of the all-seeing eye drawn over the heads of the men in the picture. I flipped it over. There was something written on the back. It was clearly Agatha's handwriting: 'Edward Grant. 32 High St. Hawkhurst, Kent.'

"It's the family that assumed control of the house after Charles Duvall died," I said. "There must be something at this address. Maybe Agatha hid the journal there."

Just then, we heard the sound of a glass bottle being kicked across the floor, outside in the hall. We both froze and listened. Again, the sound of a glass bottle rolling across the floor.

"What is that?" asked Theresa.

I quickly put everything back into the backpack and put it on. I motioned for Theresa to come closer and we both huddled next to the door. I opened the door and peered outside. The hallway was dark. One of the bulbs in the ceiling flickered on and off. I grabbed Theresa's hand and we hurried out of the room, back towards the stairs. Something made a loud noise behind us and we began running. We ran up the stairs and back into the warehouse.

"Something was following us, Andrew," Theresa said. "Did you see it?"

"No. I was too busy running," I said.

"How did they get into the building? This warehouse is completely secured."

"Call campus security," I said.

"And tell them what, exactly. We're trying to locate an artifact that was stolen from our find and we think we're being chased by a demon? Think, Andrew."

"Well, I think we should leave, right now. Do you have a car?"

"It's parked outside the faculty office building. We'll have to run across campus."

"I think that's better than staying here. We should make a run for it."

Just then, something tried to pull the door open. Theresa and I practically panicked.

"The fire exit," she said. "On the other side of the room."

We ran as quickly as we could across the room and out

the fire exit. It was dark and getting cold. The fall air was crisp. I could see my breath in the air. We ran across campus to the faculty parking lot.

We ran past a few cars. All of a sudden, a car alarm went off behind us, then another, and another. We ran until we nearly fainted. We found Theresa's car and jumped in.

"Hurry Hurry! Let's go!" I yelled.

More car alarms went off. Then Theresa fired up the engine and we pulled out of the parking lot at break neck speed.

"What the hell was all of that, Andrew?" screamed Theresa.

"I have no idea, but drive faster."

"Where to?"

"My apartment."

Theresa broke nearly every driving law there was getting us back to my apartment. Once there, we quickly ran inside. I immediately went to my bookcase and pulled out a very large dictionary.

"What's that? Theresa said.

I opened it and pulled out a 40 caliber pistol and clip and put them in my pocket.

"Protection," I said. "Just in case."

I looked out the window to see if there was anyone outside. It looked clear.

"I've had enough excitement for one night, Andrew," Theresa said. "I'm going home. Call me tomorrow if you need anything else. And bring that journal back within 24 hours or it will be both our hides."

"I will," I said. "And thank you."

I gave Theresa a very long hug and we said our goodbyes.

I placed the backpack on the dining table and removed all of the contents. Whatever answers were in Agatha's research I had to find them as quickly as possible. I opened Agatha's laptop. When the screen lit up, it asked for a password. Of course, she would keep her laptop password protected. I just closed the laptop and thought about everything Agatha had told me while she was alive.

I thought about the note in her pocket the police found the day that she was murdered; the one with my name on it. I knew there was something she wanted to tell me. I thought of the note she left the morning after we made love and the picture of the fire station. I opened the laptop and typed "burnitdown" in the password space. The computer unlocked.

There were several items right on the desktop, so I began opening them one after another. It was the same information that was in the manilla envelope she gave me. I read through them all, but there was nothing new in any of the notes. I looked at the photograph of Edward Grant and his family. I turned it over and read the address. In the morning, I'd have to go out there and have a look. It was late. I decided to get some rest.

∼

In the morning I took the train to Kent. From there, I phoned a cab and had the driver take me to the address on the back of the photograph. The cab took me out into the country to an old, abandoned country home. I got out and the cab left.

The house was in disarray. It had apparently been abandoned for decades. The house was completely boarded up. There was no way inside, so I had a look around back. In the distance, on the other side of a field, was a small barn. I decided to have a look in there. I got an eerie feeling as I crossed the field. This house seemed to have horrors of its own.

I walked over to the barn. There were no doors. It was wide open to the elements and filled with discarded furniture and other odds and ends. I searched through the wreckage.

Furniture was piled up on top of each other. I made my way further into the barn. It was cramped, but I could still make my way through. A bit further in, buried underneath a table, was an old French armoire. My heart beat and my head swooned the moment I saw it. I immediately felt compelled to dig it out and bring it home with me. It took some work, but I managed drag it out into the open. It was old and worn and painted a subtle shade of green. It was feminine and beautiful. 'This must have belonged to her,' I thought. 'The woman in my dreams.' I had suspected for a while now that the woman who had been haunting my mind and imagination was Elizabeth Colt. This seemed to confirm it. This armoire must have been removed from the house after she died. This armoire was hers. She was real. I rubbed my hand on it. It had to go in the master bedroom. In the corner by the window, just past the bed.

I decided to look around for anything else that I felt a connection to. I walked further in moving pieces of furniture out of my way as I went along. I was nearing the back of the barn when I saw them. A very old baby crib, barely holding itself together, its white paint flaking off. And behind it, piled upside down on top of a dresser against the back wall of the barn, a chaise lounge. My heart and head began to throb as soon as I saw them and my mind became possessed with the desire to bring them back to the house with me. The feeling was palpable. These items were very close to Elizabeth's heart. Things she felt a strong connection to. I made my way to the back of the barn and began digging out the chaise lounge. I carefully dragged it out into the open. It was a 1920's art nouveau chaise lounge with red velvet upholstery and a mahogany frame. A very classic and elegant style. But now it was old. It had been exposed to the elements for years. The frame was decrepit with age. The upholstery was worn and filled with holes. It was haunting to look at. But it was perfect. It belonged in the parlor. It needed to be there.

I went back into the barn to get the baby crib. Just the sight of it nearly brought me to tears. My heart was filled with anguish and heartache. It must have been Allison's crib. Elizabeth's infant daughter who died after only 18 months. I felt an overwhelming desire to get it into the house as quickly as possible. It belonged in the upstairs guest room. The room above the parlor that I had been using as my temporary sleeping quarters. I slowly and carefully moved the crib out into the open. It was so fragile that it felt like it could collapse at any moment. I dragged all three pieces out of the barn and placed them next to each other. They were terrifying to look at. But they held a certain beauty when you looked at them together. A woman's sensibilities. Very feminine and elegant. I could not leave here without them. I had to bring them home with me.

I went back into the barn to look for the journal. I started moving into the back corner of the barn. Buried in the corner was a small dresser. And on top of the dresser was an old Victrola. My heart began to thud the moment I saw it. It nearly beat right out of my chest. I climbed over some furniture and into the back corner. The Victrola was still in one piece. It hardly looked damaged at all; old and filled with cobwebs, but entirely intact.

I wound the crank to see if it still worked, and as I did, I could feel Elizabeth's hand on the crank with mine. I felt a huge rush of emotion and pain in that very instant and my heart filled with torment. I had to step back and catch my breath. I looked and there was an old record on the turntable. 'East St Louis Toodle-oo,' by Duke Ellington.

I lifted and carried the Victrola out of the barn and placed it with the rest of the furniture. I felt such sadness and pain just looking at them. I wondered what Elizabeth Colt was like while she were alive. And I wondered what happened to her and her daughter at the end of their lives. After having read the horrors of what happened in that house, I could only imagine.

I closed my eyes and tried to imagine what she was like. Slowly an image drifted into my mind. I saw a woman in a field carrying a bouquet of flowers. I saw her dancing in the parlor. I saw her laying on the chaise lounge, holding a baby, listening to music. They were so happy. So beautiful. Then the pounding in my head and heart began again and all I felt was pain and torment. I started to cry. I couldn't hold back the tears it was so horrible and sad. I opened my eyes. What happened to this woman and child? How did Agatha know about this place? Why did she lead me out here?

I went back into the barn to search for the journal. I wandered around looking everywhere I possibly could. I had no idea where to look, so I just looked through everything an inch at a time. I was nearing the wall of barn when my head began to throb. I felt a flash of pain in my mind and I began having visions. I saw a horrible man torturing someone. He was ripping a man's flesh off. Stabbing him in the leg. Slashing his face with a knife. It was horrific. I looked around at all of the furniture. I stepped forward and the sensation grew stronger. I dark and evil force. I dug through the furniture in the barn moving lamps and tables out of the way.

On the floor of the barn, next to the wall, lay a music

box. It was a clown holding a balloon. A child's toy perhaps. It was quite large. I picked it up and immediately felt a stabbing sensation in my head. I turned it over. On the bottom was a drawing of the all-seeing eye. The eye with beams of light shining down from it. Agatha must have drawn it. I took out my pocket knife and unscrewed the bottom. Inside was the journal. It was bound together with several pieces of paper with a thick rubber band. Agatha's notes. She had hidden it in this barn. I put it inside my jacket pocket.

I wondered if she knew it was Elizabeth; the ghost that's been haunting us. I wondered if the ghost was good or evil. But did I care? She seemed to be in utter torment. Maybe she had every right to be angry.

I wondered if Agatha was right and this being was demonic; here to cause the end of the world. I wondered if that would be so bad. What have we actually done to the world? Maybe we deserved it.

I decided to call a lorry to come pick me up and bring the furniture back to the house. I still felt an overwhelming desire to get the furniture into the house as quickly as possible. It was a need. When the lorry arrived, the driver and I loaded the furniture into the bed and we drove back to the house. When we arrived at the house, I noticed that the front door had been taped shut by the police. The driver pulled into the driveway and we unloaded the furniture. I paid the driver an extra £50 to leave me the dolly and we parted ways.

6

"**B**reak the Lock."

As soon as the lorry was gone, I felt an overwhelming urge to get the furniture into the house as quickly as possible. I went around back to the patio. The doors were taped shut by the police. I broke the tape, opened the door, and walked inside.

"Hello?" I called out. I walked into the foyer. "Hello?' I called out again.

The house was empty. I went outside and strapped the French armoire to the dolly. I rolled it in through the kitchen and into the foyer. I rolled it through the foyer to the bottom of the stairs. I turned at the foot of the stairs and started to pull it up. The armoire was quite heavy, but I heaved and pulled the dolly up the stairs one step at a time. Once at the top, I pulled the dolly down the hall and into the master bedroom. I unstrapped the armoire from the dolly and moved it into the far corner of the room.

Once the armoire was in place, I felt a heartbeat

emanate from the house. It seemed to shake the entire floor. And I felt a woman's presence in the room. It was Elizabeth. I could feel her emotions. Then she appeared in front of me. An apparition. She seemed happy to have her favorite dresser back in her room. She motioned for to me to move it. It wasn't quite in the right position. I felt compelled to listen to her. She directed and I followed. I moved it slightly closer to the window. I angled it more towards the wall. She stopped me and clapped her hands. Then she climbed on top of the four poster bed and disappeared. After she had gone, I looked at the bed and the armoire together. The armoire perfectly matched the aesthetic of the room.

I hurried back outside to get the baby crib. I loaded the crib onto the dolly. It was so fragile I had to mover very slowly as not to damage it. It was considerably lighter than the armoire, so I was able to take my time and very gingerly wheel it up the steps of the stairs one step at a time. The closer I got to the upstairs guest room, the faster my heart pounded. I brought the crib into the guest room, moved the bed out of the way, and placed the crib in the center of the room. As soon as it was in position, I heard a baby's laughter. I little girl. Then Elizabeth appeared. She picked up the baby, spun her around in the air, and hugged her. She was so joyful. They both were. I felt all the love her mother gave to young Allison tugging at my heart strings. Then the feeling turned pitch black and I was filled with torment and pain. Rainclouds appeared outside the windows and a storm of thunder and lightning formed. Anger filled the air. Elizabeth screamed and disappeared. I felt such an immense sense of torment and sorrow that it brought me to tears.

I struggled to regain control of my senses. My body shook, but I had to get back outside. I had to get the Chaise lounge into the house as quickly as possible. I was being driven by her emotions. It needed to be in the parlor. I grabbed the dolly and nearly ran back out to the driveway. Once I saw the chaise, a flood of emotions ran through me. They were angry and powerful. Full of tears and pain. It had begun to rain and it came down as I strapped the chaise lounge to the dolly and rushed back into the house. I could feel her pulling me toward the parlor, telling me to move faster. Once I was in the room, she appeared again. She was dressed in satin pajamas with slippers on, carrying a hair brush.

"Place it right her," she said and I heard her voice as clear as if she were standing in the room with me. She seemed impatient, even anxious.

I wheeled the chaise into the center of the parlor and unstrapped it from the dolly. I lifted it up and placed it at an angle on the oriental rug in front of the fireplace. She quickly shooed me back outside. She needed her Victrola.

I ran back outside into the rain. I placed the dolly next to the door on the patio and returned to the driveway to get the Victrola. Lightning flashed in the sky. And there she was again, standing beside me.

"Bring it this way, quickly now," she commanded. "Please hurry. I can't wait."

Then she ran inside the house. I carried the Victrola through the house and into the parlor.

"Right here," she said. And she pointed at the far end of the chaise lounge near the fireplace. I set the Victrola down on the floor, grabbed an end table from next to the divan, and set it next to the chaise lounge. Then I picked up the Victrola and placed it on top of the end table.

She stood and watched me the whole time. She put her hand to her chin, and thought. Then she directed me to turn the Victrola slightly in a counterclockwise motion. So I did. She put up her hand and said, "Stop."

She giggled and laughed, but what I felt was not happiness. She seemed angry and malevolent.

"I have to run upstairs to change clothes," she said and she disappeared.

I decided to follow her. I went upstairs to the master bedroom and looked at the French Armoire. She was standing in front of it changing her clothes. She saw me and threw her hair brush at me.

"Get out of here, you pervert," she said playfully.

I left the room and closed the door.

"I'll be out in a minute," I heard her voice say through the door. Her voice was eerie and haunting. "Go check on Allison," she said.

I didn't know what to do, so I simply followed her commands and did as she said. I went to Allison's room and looked inside the crib. Moments later she appeared in the room wearing a slinky black negligee. She reached into the crib, picked up baby Allison, and ran downstairs. I followed her back into the parlor. She jumped onto the chaise lounge, holding Allison in her lap. She picked up a record from the floor and put it on the turntable. She wound the crank and giggled in excitement. The music started. In moments, a woman's vocals filled the air:

"I used to have a perfect sweetheart. Not a real one, just a dream. A wonderful vision of us as a team. Can you imagine how I feel now? Love is real now. Its ideal. You're just what I wanted and now it's nice to live. Paradise to live. I know why I've waited. Know why I've been blue. I've prayed each night for someone exactly like you."

Elizabeth laughed and bopped her head. She played with baby Allison. She looked at me. Her face was distorted and ugly.

"Don't worry, you'll get your turn later, mister," she said and dropped a wink.

Then she disappeared and the music stopped.

I sat on the divan and just stared at the chaise lounge. I got up and went from room to room looking at each piece of furniture. They were haunting, yet beautiful. I felt a pulse emanating from the house; from the room behind the door in the cellar.

∽

I still hadn't read Agatha's notes. I went into the study, took the journal out of my pocket, and placed it on the desk. What had she uncovered that cost her her life? Why did she say that they chose me to open the door? I had to know. I removed the rubber band and looked through all of the papers. On top, there was a newspaper clipping with a photograph of the entire Duvall household. There were seven people in the photograph. Below the photograph, in the caption, it listed their names. The Duvall family stood to the left and the servants stood to the right. Agatha had circled three people and three names. She circled a young boy of about ten years of age, standing in front. In the caption she circled the name Charles Duvall. She circled a young girl who looked to be about the same age as young Charles, standing a few paces away from him, to the right amongst the servants. In the caption Agatha circled the name Elizabeth Colt. Lastly, she circled one of the adult female servants. In the caption, she drew several circles around the name. Her name was Margaret Colt. Elizabeth's mother. Elizabeth was the daughter of one of the servants.

I read through Agatha's notes. Apparently, Margaret Colt was a servant in the Duvall household. And she lived there with her daughter Elizabeth. Elizabeth was two years younger than Charles and they were most likely childhood friends. They grew up together. There were strict rules about family and children interacting with the servants and their children in those days. In a household filled with blood and murder it must have been dangerous. Agatha thought the body they found in the carriage house might be that of Margaret Colt.

I turned to the next page in Agatha's notes. She had drawn a diagram of two family trees. One was of my own family and the other was of the Duvall family. Apparently, four generations ago, one of my distant relatives was a cousin of Frederick Duvall. Charles and I were related. According to Agatha's notes, that's why the Pretorians chose me to open the door. She believed that the door could only be opened by a blood relative of Charles Duvall.

On the next page, there was a description of what happened in the house just prior to the door being sealed. According to Agatha, Charles' relatives were against his marriage to Elizabeth Colt. They were all Praetorians and they couldn't allow any outsiders into the family. So, one Christmas they all came to the house. They took Elizabeth and her infant daughter into the room in the cellar that is blocked by the door. They nailed Elizabeth to the wall with metal spikes and began a ritual. They broke the arms, legs, and neck of Elizabeth's infant daughter, Allison. They cut out the infant's heart and burned it, right in front of Elizabeth as she screamed in agony. Then they flayed the skin from Elizabeth's arms and torso while she was still alive, exposing her ribs, chest, and still beating heart. They formed a circle and began reciting incantations to call forth the Babylonian Demon that they worshipped. They continued to recite the incantations until Elizabeth's heart stopped. Then they cut out Elizabeth's heart and burned it.

A copy of the hand written note, the one I saw in the secretary the day we opened the closet upstairs, was last. In it, Charles's wrote: "I loved her. She was my life. And you robbed me of her. So, I will rob you of your god. I curse you all. Damn you all to hell." It was Charles Duvall who poured molten lead into the lock sealing the door shut.

According to what Agatha had translated from the journals, Charles performed his own ritual and cursed the door, then he committed suicide. And according to the notes Charles wrote in the journal, the curse can only be lifted by family blood. My blood, apparently.

"My god," I said aloud.

On the back of the page there was a note from Agatha. In it, she again begged me not to open the door. That if I did it would bring about the end of the world.

I went into the billiard room, to the bar, and poured myself a drink. I sat there pondering the horrors of the home. A few moments later, my cell phone rang.

"Hello?" I said.

"Andrew, it's Chad." It was Chad my friend and colleague at the firm.

"Hello, Chad. What is it?"

"I'm afraid I've got some bad news. The partners heard about what happened to Agatha. The police stopped by the office this afternoon and asked some questions. Well, they seem to think that you are somehow involved. The firm doesn't want it to go to press. But, they're taking the house away from you. They've nullified the contract. They're going to sell it on the market for £2.2 million next month. I'm sorry ol' chum. It's bad news all around, I'm afraid."

I just hung up the phone and poured myself another drink. I closed my eyes and tried to concentrate. I sat at the bar contemplating what Agatha had written in her notes. And as I stood there, I slowly realized that I could hear music. Jazz music playing on a Victrola. It sounded real. Duke Ellington, 'East St. Louis Toodle-oo.' It was coming from the parlor. I followed the sound into the room.

The record on the Victrola was spinning. Elizabeth was on the floor in front of the chaise lounge, sobbing. She looked up at me and screamed:

"WHY?"

Then she became a black cloud of anger and fury and crashed through the French Doors into the dining room. The doors exploded and glass and wood flew through the air. The Victrola stopped. A few moments later, the music began again. It had moved down into the cellar. Into the room underneath the parlor; the room blocked by the ancient black door. It was the same song by Duke Ellington. Only it sounded like it was playing at half speed on a warped turntable. The volume kept going in and out and the music was distorted. A cold chill filled the air. The entire house must have dropped 20 degrees. Lightning shone through the windows and a clap of thunder filled the air. The furnace kicked on and the blower kicked in. I got lightheaded and started to faint. I stumbled over to the chaise lounge to lie down. The room spun in circles. I saw black and passed out.

In my slumber I began to have a nightmare. I saw Amanda standing in a circle with several of the partners from the firm. They were all wearing purple robes with purple and white vestments, chanting in unison. Mr. George was there, as was Mr. Douglas. So was Shelly, the secretary, and Earl, the copy boy. They all stood around a young girl who was naked and tied to an alter. They all chanted, 'Eso To Gat Ether Hume,' over and over again. Amanda raised a silver dagger and stabbed the young girl in the chest. The young girl screamed and blood dripped over the alter. The chanting grew louder and faster. 'Eso To Gat Ether Hume,' they repeated over and over again as Amanda cut out the young girl's heart and placed it into a fire, burning it. They became lost in a frenzy as the heart burned in the flames. I could hear something pounding, pounding, pounding on the door in the cellar.

I awoke in the middle of the night. The rain had stopped. The full moon shone through the windows. I could still see the image of the ritual in my mind. My muscles twitched. Then I felt Elizabeth's presence. My heart warmed. I felt her love. I heard the sound of music drifting up from the cellar; from the room behind the door:

"Falling in love again. Never wanted to. What am I to do? Can't help it. Love's always been my game. Play it how I may. I was made that way. Can't help it. Men cluster to me like moths around a flame. And if their wings burn. I know I'm not to blame. Falling in love again. Never wanted to. What's a girl to do. I can't help it."

I slowly walked around the parlor, listening to the music. Then I heard her laugh. It echoed through the floor from the room below. I placed my hand on the mantel of the fireplace and closed my eyes. I could see her in my mind. She was so beautiful. So warm. She beckoned me to come forward. I felt compelled to follow her. I tried to open my eyes, but she stopped me.

"No," she said, shaking her head. "Come to me."

I kept my eyes closed. She led and I followed. I followed her presence out of the parlor and into the foyer. She was leading me to the cellar. I crossed the foyer to the top of the stairs. I followed her one step at a time, down, down, down, into the darkness.

Once at the bottom, I heard the furnace ignite and the blower kick in. Air rushed through the ductwork. I felt the heat of the furnace waft around me. The furnace growled a demonic growl as it billowed heat. Sweat began to drip from my forehead. The music stopped. I continued forward. I felt the door next to me. I felt the hewn timbers. I felt the iron ring. I stopped and lowered myself to the floor. I felt the keyhole.

"Look," she commanded.

I opened my eyes. Swirls of pink and purple ethereal light bled through the keyhole and filled the air. I stared at the impenetrable lock that I tried so many times to break through. I crouched in front of the door, wondering what lie behind it. I placed my hand into the pink and purple light, watching the dust sift through it. I put my ear against the door and listened. She was on the other side. I heard her cross the room and put on another record. The music drifted through the air and into my senses:

"You were meant for me. And I was meant for you. Nature fashioned you and when she was done, you were all of the sweet things rolled up in one. You're like a plaintive melody, that never lets me be. But I'm content. The angels must have sent you and they meant you just for me."

The words filled my mind and heart. Wearily, I placed my eye in front of the keyhole, to look in. The light went black.

BOOM! Something pounded the door so hard it knocked me back. The iron ring shook. It seemed the entire house shook from its force.

"Let me out," she whispered. "Break the lock."

I was mesmerized by the sound of her voice. I was captivated by her beauty. I searched around in the darkness and felt a bag. One of the tool bags that the mysterious locksmith brought with him. He must have left it behind. I opened it and searched inside. I found a set of lock picks. I fumbled in the dark and put pick to lock, over and over again. I could feel the tumbler and I felt it move.

BOOM! Another pound on the door. Then the pink and purple light shone through the keyhole again. She beckoned me forward, gently curling her index finger.

"Look," she beckoned.

I looked through the keyhole and there she was, as real as if she were alive, standing there naked, wearing thigh

high patent leather boots, holding a bullwhip. I could smell her perfume. It was intoxicating.

"Open the door," she commanded. And she cracked the whip.

The music played as I dumbly felt for the lock pick trying to fit it into the keyhole. Sweat poured off my brow and ran down my nose before dripping onto the dusty floor of the cellar. The furnace billowed heat, so cloying, smothering me in its embrace. I could barely see my hands in front of me in the dim, pale light of the moon that entered from the door at the top of the stairs. I was beyond fear. I was beyond temptation. I had to have her. I was desperate to have her or else lose my sanity.

Sealed in her vault, she danced. I could hear her laughing. I could smell her perfume. All I could see was the pale beam of pink and purple light drifting out from the keyhole. She was on the other side.

Madly, I pounded the intolerable door. I spat at the impenetrable lock. And I shrieked at the top of my lungs, "I must have you!" into the distant echoes of the night. I cried as I vainly fit pick to lock again and again, trying to turn the tumbler, to free the door, and gain entry into her paradise; her forbidden Eden. It was there I wanted to dwell. It was there I wanted to spend the rest of my life; with her. My hands trembled and I dripped with sweat, teeth clenched, fumbling in the dark.

I felt a piece of debris fall off the tumbler and I heard the lock click. Everything went silent. The light went black. And time stood still. Nothing stirred. Not even the dust. I looked at the glowing flames of the furnace. I could feel the heat. But the flames did not move. Then the blower kicked in and woke me from my trance. The black door stared back at me.

A swirling cloud of black smoke with green eyes engulfed me.

ACKNOWLEDGMENTS

I would like to thank my parents for being the reason I am here and for giving me everything I have in my life. I learned everything from my parents and I am humbled to be the son of such exceptional people. I hope that we all live for many more years to come. And I hope that all of you can thank those who gave you life and brought you into this world.

    Peace and Justice.

Musical references:
    Lambert Murphy - Lonesome That's All - 1919.
    Josephine Baker - Bye Bye Blackbird - 1926.
    Ted Fio Rito - (I Don't Stand) A Ghost Of A Chance With You (Vera Van, vocal) - 1933.
    Ruth Etting - Exactly Like You - 1929.
    Duke Ellington and his Kentucky Club Orchestra - East St. Louis Toodle-Oo - 1927.
    Marlene Dietrich - Falling in Love Again - 1930.
    Willie Creager & His Orchestra - You Were Meant For Me - 1929.

Cover Design by Leo Alexander Sakharov.
PNG art by PNGWAV.com

ABOUT THE AUTHOR

Leo Alexander Sakharov is an underground artist from Detroit, Michigan. He studied Literature, Drama, and Creative Writing at Henry Ford College in Dearborn, the University of Michigan in Ann Arbor - with a summer abroad at St. Peter's College at the University of Oxford - and at the University of British Columbia in Vancouver.

Sakharov's background is in Comparative Literature and Drama in the English language predominately by artists from the United States, England, and Canada. He has studied several genres of Literature and Drama from the Greek Tragedies, to Medieval Literature and the Arthurian Legends, to the Modernists and Postmodernists, to Gen X Literature and Graphic Narrative.

Sakharov has also worked professionally as a Theatre Technical Director and Scenic Designer at several local theatres, colleges, and universities.

He lives with his family just outside the city of Detroit.
This is his second book.

Made in the USA
Monee, IL
04 November 2020